The Star Probe

"He'll set the ship down right here," Dan said. "Put yourself in the Alien's place. If you were orbiting a desolate planet that had one rather large blue bubble on it, where would you land?"

"The bubble," Jennie agreed. "We'd better break out the red carpet, then. It's best not to antagonize creatures from Outer Space. So my old mother always told me..."

"Mother!" Dan sniffed. "You no more had a *mother* than I did. Than any of us!"

AN EXERCISE FOR MADMEN

Barbara Paul

AN EXERCISE FOR MADMEN

BARBARA PAUL

A BERKLEY BOOK
published by
BERKLEY PUBLISHING CORPORATION

Berkley Publishing Corporation
200 Madison Avenue
New York, New York 10016

SBN 425-03809-2

BERKLEY MEDALLION BOOKS are published by
Berkley Publishing Corporation
200 Madison Avenue
New York, N. Y. 10016

BERKLEY MEDALLION BOOK ® TM 757,375

Printed in the United States of America

Berkley Edition, July, 1978

AN EXERCISE FOR
MADMEN

Part I

Chorus

A tongue without reins,
defiance, unwisdom—
their end is disaster.
But the life of quiet good,
the wisdom that accepts—
these abide unshaken,
preserving, sustaining
the houses of men.
                    —Euripides
                    The Bacchae

The computer flashboard sat waiting patiently for her next deathless pronouncement.

Pathetic fallacy, thought Jennie Geiss. Patience is a human quality, not a mechanical one.

Twenty minutes left. Not much done today, and at eleven o'clock she would have to yield the use of the computer to someone else. Old Dr. Tirsos, probably.

She cleared her throat and watched the design the sound made on the flashboard. Then she began to speak.

> So many discoveries have come from the Pythia Medical Research Project that some of the Earth's inhabitants have already forgotten what those early contributions were. The myoelectrically controlled exoskeleton for paraplegics. The Braningan method for stimulating the reserve half of the brain in stroke victims. The elimination of mongolism through introducing repressor molecules into the proper places on the DNA chain. All these now-standard medical procedures first came from Pythia.

Jennie watched her words flashed on the computer board as she spoke them. Simultaneously the voicewriter was typing those same words (original, two carbons) for her to take with her. She grunted. The writing was bad. An exoskeleton isn't a "medical procedure," it's a *thing*. That would have to be changed.

But not today.

Jennie jammed her papers into her already full briefcase and left the cubicle that separated "her" part of the computer from the rest of the monster. Old Dr. Tirsos was waiting in the hall.

"You still have fifteen minutes," he said.

"Talked out." She smiled brightly. "Go ahead."

He nodded and entered the cubicle with more dignity than the occasion would seem to warrant. Quite a gift, dignity.

A group of technicians was removing the metal siding from another part of the computer. Jennie had almost passed them by when she saw that one of the technicians was Jacob, who had been at Pythia almost as long as Jennie had.

"Hello, Jacob," she said, pausing. "How's it going?"

Jacob reached for the slate and stylus attached to his utility belt and scribbled one word.

Earache, Jennie read. "Oh, I'm sorry," she said, concerned. "I hope it's not too bad."

A hairy arm snaked around her neck and she found herself caught in a warm, animal hug.

"Have you seen your doctor?" she asked.

One o'clock, Jacob wrote on the slate.

"Well, he'll fix you up. Do you feel well enough to be working?"

Jacob nodded vigorously and turned back to his job. Jennie walked on, musing. For the hundredth time she wondered why the Pythian geniuses had never been able to come up with a surgical procedure that would enable the chimps to talk.

Inside the cubicle, Dr. Tirsos sat staring at the controls of the computer he was supposed to be using.

He was worrying about Jennie Geiss.

He knew that too-bright smile, that too-cheery greeting—the first signs that Jennie's none-too-sturdy defense mechanisms were soon going to need bolstering. It had happened before.

His gray head jerked in annoyance. He should have insisted that she return to Earth eight years ago. But no, his own curiosity had betrayed the girl.

—There it was again: that pain in the lumbar region. He had had a complete physical last week; the results had told him he wasn't as young as he used to be. This was hardly news; Dr. Tirsos was the oldest person on Pythia.

He made a mental note to have another examination tomorrow. At his age a weekly check-up wouldn't be extreme.

Pythia was one of Mother Necessity's many offspring.

The Earth's inhabitants had long been growing increasingly frightened of the research being done in infectious diseases, germ warfare, and the medical uses of radiation—and with some justification. As far back as 1954, Clement Attlee had undoubtedly spoken aloud the fears of a great number of people when he told the House of Commons (on April Fool's Day) that civilization was at stake. "The Greek civilization was suddenly overwhelmed by the barbarians," he'd said. "With us, the danger comes from the scientists." When this distrust of science showed little sign of abating, it gradually became clear that what was needed was an isolated place where research could continue uninterrupted without any immediate danger to human life. In short, another planet.

Since the medical colony would be dealing with materials and techniques that could prove harmful to life if they ever got out of control, the problem then became one of selecting a planet that was *not* likely to be life-supporting. An artificial environment would be constructed, and the researchers could proceed without any limitations except normal precautions for their own safety.

All the usable planets and asteroids in the solar system had already been pressed into service, either as data-gathering stations or as mining operations. Several thousand asteroids were too small or too something, while some of the planets, such as Jupiter, were unthinkable. The clouds of Venus were being seeded to change that planet's atmosphere to one more nearly like that of Earth, but when Venus eventually became habitable, it would be colonized. And Proserpina, the tenth planet in Earth's star system, had turned out to be just what was expected: another ball of ice. So the search for a safe base of operations had been extended into star systems within a range of five parsecs.

Since the discovery of anthropoid life on two of the

planets orbiting Epsilon Eridani, earthmen had begun thinking "outward" again. An elaborate network of relay stations had made delayed voice-messages possible among the three known inhabited planets, but actual visits to Epsilon Eridani still lay in the future. Once Earth had begun sending out exploratory probes on a regular basis, other types of life had been uncovered, even a form of vegetation based on nitrogen and boron. Any planet that showed signs of developing life was to be ruled out as a base for the medical research colony.

The best possibility had turned out to be right next door in the galaxy, a small planet orbiting Alpha Centauri—4.3 light years away. Alpha Centauri was part of a triple star system, with the two larger bodies revolving around each other in an orbit with a semimajor axis of only about twenty astronomical units. The large eccentricity of this binary orbit made it impossible for the system's planets to remain in the habitable zone for lengthy periods. Therefore there was no well-evolved life to be threatened.

The colonists were not dedicated to developing a new culture but rather to preserving the one they brought with them from Earth, and, it was hoped, to improving upon one part of it. So Pythia operated on a system of rhythmic cycles intended to recreate the familiar. Although research continued around the clock, darkness alternated with light (thus making the "night people" happy). Earth's seasons were reproduced, as well as Earth's landscape—as much of it as there was room for inside the artificial environment, which covered only a small part of the planet's total surface area. The design engineers kept in mind at all times they were responsible for reproducing an ecosystem that would distract the scientists as little as possible. This meant a *known* way of life, one that could be lived without interfering with the real work at hand.

"Whenever you're feeling down," Jennie's tutor had once told her, "try swimming. It helps."

Jennie took the moveway to the extreme northern edge of the settlement, where the recreational facilities were located.

After she had changed, she spotted Claude Billings, a dermatologist, sitting on the side of the pool paddling his feet in the water. Jennie touched him lightly on the shoulder and sat down beside him.

"Jen. How's the latest best-seller coming?"

"Rehash of the first two."

"Oh, c'mon."

"The first part anyway. Introductory material for those imaginary readers who never heard of Pythia. I thought this time I'd concentrate on the people here."

"An exposé?"

Jennie laughed. "I wish there were something *to* expose. No, I just think the last thing Earth needs right now is another history of what's been done on Pythia. In layman's language, yet."

"But told by a layman actually living on Pythia. That should always have a special appeal to Earth readers."

"You sound like the publicity blurbs my publisher sends out. Truth is, I wrote one book twice and I just don't want to do it again. My publisher agrees a book of word-portraits would probably sell quite well. People on Earth are naturally nosey about people on Pythia."

"Is it important to you? That the book sells well, I mean."

"Certainly! The more I can get stashed away in the bank the better. Remember, I've never been to Earth. I'll probably need a lot of time to adjust. And I'll have to have something to live on while I'm doing it."

"That's right, I'd forgotten. You've lived your entire life here, haven't you?"

"Yes." There was a slight edge to her voice.

"Well," Claude hastened to say, "arriving on Earth with your fortune already made isn't going to hurt you."

"Oh, I don't have all that much money. The publisher takes a big hunk, and then Pythia gets a slice—as my legal employer under whose auspices the books were written. I get what's left, but I have to pay transmission costs out of that."

"Transmission costs? You mean the cost of transmitting the text from Pythia through the relays to your publisher on Earth?"

"Yup."

"That doesn't seem fair. Pythia should pay it."

"I couldn't agree more."

They watched the swimmers for a while. Then Claude asked, "Have you decided whom you're going to write about?"

"Dr. Tirsos, of course. Thalia Boyd. And I'd like to devote a chapter to Dan."

Claude thought this over. "Yes," he finally said, "that's good. I think people should understand about Dan."

Just then the pagemaster strapped to his wrist *bleeped!* with an urgency that startled them both. "Oh, hell," Claude said. "I just got here."

Claude Billings was thinking of Jennie as he jogged back to the moveway. She had been an unhappy adolescent when he arrived at Pythia eight years earlier, but she had since developed into an attractive woman. There was always an air of melancholy about her, though—understandable, of course, since she didn't really belong on Pythia.

He wondered about her private life. He knew she'd broken off a long-standing love affair a few months ago. But she hadn't formed any new alliances since then. Did that mean she was off men?

Then he remembered the way she'd touched his shoulder as she sat down beside him. Claude smiled.

Jennie watched Claude jog away, and then slipped into the pool.

Water therapy. Back-to-the-artificial-womb time.

The pool was located in the foothills of the one mountain that had been enclosed within the artificial environment. The pool was man-made, but the mountain was authentic enough to satisfy anybody's back-to-nature urges. Jennie swam lazily for a while and then floated on her back, looking at Pythia's artificial sky.

She wondered what a cloud looked like, *really* looked like. She had seen photographs of Earth's clouds, of course.

To someone who had seen nothing but the unbroken blue of Pythia's simulated heavens, clouds seemed like imperfections in a fabric. But too many earthmen had written poetry about clouds for that to be true.

Unexpectedly, Jennie's head encountered an obstacle: someone else's head. The two swimmers laughed and apologized. As Jennie dog-paddled away she was surprised to see how many people were in the pool. They must have come in while she was daydreaming about clouds.

She pulled herself out of the pool and looked down to see a silver streak headed straight for her. A head broke the surface at the edge of the pool: it belonged to Sam Flaherty, a lean, sandy-haired young man engaged in a life-long love affair with himself.

"Hi," Sam said as he hauled himself up beside her. "Want to race?"

"With you? Not on your life."

Sam laughed easily and stretched out on his back. "Don't blame you. Nobody else will race me either."

"Wonder why," said Jennie dryly.

"I can't imagine," Sam answered, wiggling his webbed hands and feet. "There's a lot more to swimming than having built-in flippers. Coordination, endurance—"

"Oh, Sam," sighed Jennie. "You're just fishing for compliments." Sam could swim three laps in a race while a normal was still laboring on his first.

"Just joking," Sam said. "I know you normies don't like to race. You feel at a disadvantage."

Jennie struggled against her annoyance, but took the bait anyway. "Well, aren't we?"

"Look, don't get sore at me. It's not my fault I was given webbing and you weren't. But I imagine it does get to you after a while." He pretended a detached interest. "What does it feel like, Jennie, having nothing but your natural body? Doesn't it make you feel, well, underequipped?"

"Sometimes it makes me feel angry," Jennie answered slowly. "Like right now."

Sam grinned at her. "Just an outward manifestation of your inherent fear of competition."

"Nobody likes unfair competition." Jennie got to her feet.

"And right now, Sam, I don't much like *you*."

She heard him laughing at her as she walked away.

Sam Flaherty experienced a rare twinge of conscience.

He shouldn't have baited Jennie; it *wasn't* fair. She'd always been decent to him; most of the normies would have nothing to do with him.

But damn it, she was such a patsy! Why didn't she tell him to go to hell, the way everybody else did? He couldn't stand people who were determined to be nice to him. As if he were some sort of freak. It was the normies who were the freaks.

Sam turned down an invitation to race—and quickly became aware that everyone within hearing distance was staring at him in surprise.

The moveway back to the settlement was crowded. Jennie located a place to sit on the center bench and found herself rubbing shoulders with two adolescents she didn't know. Where do all these people come from? They're being decanted too fast, she decided.

Too many people, too many people. No *Lebensraum*. Pythia didn't maintain construction facilities and had to depend upon prefab expansions provided by Earth. Supply ships visited Pythia at nine-year intervals, and the next one was due next year. In the meantime, the growing population of Pythia was spilling out of its normal quarters into remodeled storerooms and other makeshift living areas. Jennie stepped off the moveway earlier than necessary, just to get away from the crowd.

She was depressed. A whoopee pill might help.

The pharmacist was a chubby, good-natured man named Adelbert Phillips. With a first name like Adelbert to cope with, nobody bothered remembering "Phillips."

"Bert, what do I have left on my script?"

Adelbert punched her prescription number into the computer terminal and squinted at the small print that appeared on the screen. "Five grains of Elysium."

"Is that all?"

"That's all."

She needed four times that. "I'll take it," she said.

Bert ceremoniously removed one tablet from a container filled to the brim and dropped it into a plastic envelope. "If you want more, see a doctor."

"And where would I find a doctor around here?" she asked, completing the old joke as she left.

Adelbert wiped away a fleck of dust only he could see. He instructed the computer that Jennie Geiss had just received the last of the tranquillizer allotted her on her current prescription.

He shook his head. Trouble.

That little bit of Elysium wouldn't do her any good. What a stupid name—Elysium! They'd probably call the next one Ecstaticum.

And put Jennie on it. She could build up a tolerance to a new drug faster than anyone on Pythia. The all-time champeen. Well, thought Adelbert, all I do is dish 'em out and keep track. I don't have to decide who takes how much of what.

He laughed humorlessly. *I'm so glad I'm not an Alpha.*

Jennie Geiss's parents were a sperm-and-ova bank in New York City. She had come to Pythia as a frozen embryo fifty-four years ago; but since she hadn't been decanted until twenty-seven years after her arrival, she was now only twenty-seven. She had been part of a control group used in those early experiments with implanting supplementary hearts.

When she was five, two-thirds of the children in her embryo group underwent surgery. Half of them were given animal hearts, the other half had prosthetic mechanisms installed. Jennie's group (all surnamed Geiss for quick identification) was to grow up normally, without the benefit of surgical augmentation.

Jennie and the other Geisses were scheduled to return to Earth on the ship that arrived when they were nineteen. They were no longer needed on Pythia; and the general policy was to return normals to Earth as early as possible to allow them to build lives for themselves among others of their own kind. The ship arrived, Jennie was packed and eager to go, and then something happened that had kept her on Pythia.

She caught a cold.

The cold virus had long ago been isolated and, everyone thought, stamped out. Certainly no one on Pythia had ever had a cold. Jennie found herself being given the most *intense* intensive care ever accorded someone suffering from such a minor ailment. There was a constant parade of physicians through her sick room; every M.D. on Pythia examined her. How had she caught the cold? It was a mystery Pythia's doctors were never able to solve.

By the time she was back on her feet again, the ship had left. *Wann geht der nächste Schwan*? There wouldn't be another ship for nine years.

Once she'd recovered from the shock, Jennie started asking why she hadn't simply been given some medication and put on the ship? Everyone gave her a different answer. You were too sick. We didn't want to send the cold virus back to Earth and start that ugly business all over again. The pilot was afraid to assume responsibility for you. But it was old Dr. Tirsos who had undoubtedly told her the truth.

"We wanted to see what a cold looked like," he said.

Jennie had never forgiven them.

Dr. Thalia Boyd sat in her office puzzling out the wording of a message to Earth. Earth authorities were demanding an accounting of Pythia's intelligence-raising experiments and an explanation of why these techniques had not yet been passed on to them. The communication she had received from Earth did not come right out and accuse Pythian scientists of keeping the discovery for their own benefit, but the implication was there.

Thalia Boyd sighed. Even this far out in space it was impossible to escape Earth's bureaucracy. And as Administrative Head of Pythia Project, it was part of Thalia's job to soothe and explain. She activated the recorder and began to speak.

> *Intelligence-raising was among Pythia's first priorities, and experiments with chimpanzees are still being conducted. Since no way of stimulating the neuronal networks in adult apes has been found, the apes are treated before they are born.*

That had been one of the two experiments that made it possible to put chimpanzees to work as computer technicians.

> *Pregnant chimps are injected with pituitary growth hormones—while the brain of the fetus is still maturing. This increases the ratio of neurons to supporting glial cells. But more importantly, in the cortex the cell density and the number and length of the dendrites are increased.*
>
> *Also, the oxygen supply to the fetus is increased. The placenta stops growing toward the end of pregnancy; this is why we have never been able to use our full brain potential. The fetal brain fails to develop to its full capacity because the fetus's demand for oxygen is greater than the mother's ability to supply it. So it is the combination of pituitary growth hormones and fetal oxygenation that produces new-born chimps with increased intelligence.*
>
> *Much of the basic research in intelligence-raising had already been done before the establishment of Pythia Project. Pythia scientists concentrated on determining what additives were necessary to prevent giantism and other freak side effects.*

So much for what was being done. Now as to why Earth had not yet been given the techniques for raising the intelligence of its inhabitants.

> *Pythia has begun applying its intelligence-raising techniques to human beings. Children who have been given this treatment while still embryos implanted in artificial placentas all show signs of extremely high intelligence. But as the oldest of these children are only six years old, not enough time has passed to provide an accurate, long-range measure of the results. Pythia will be in a better position to evaluate the treatment ten years from now.*

The rest of the communication from Earth was taken up by a recurrent complaint: when do we get the artificial kidney? Prosthetic substitutes for diseased kidneys had been in use for generations, but the totally man-made kidney remained elusive. (We have interstellar travel, but we don't have the artificial kidney, grumble, grumble.) Before tackling that one, Thalia punched out Dr. Tirsos's code number on the communicator. It was several minutes before the old man's face appeared on the screen.

"I can't put off answering Earth any longer," said Thalia. "Do you have anything new about the kidney?"

"No, and we won't for some time. I don't foresee any breakthrough in the near future. The one we've installed in Dan works perfectly, of course; but then Dan's a special case. You'll just have to tell them to wait."

Thalia suppressed a groan. She was hoping Dr. Tirsos would say "We're on to something," or "Dr. So-and-So just had an idea." That at least would give her something to work with. "Well, thanks anyway."

"As long as you're on, Thalia, there's something else. How long has it been since you've seen Jennie Geiss?"

"Three or four days. Why?"

"She's on the verge of another depressive period."

"Oh, no." This time Thalia did groan.

"I'm afraid so. Can you increase her medication?"

"No. I'm pushing the limit as it is. But I'll check on her. Thanks for the tip."

Dr. Tirsos's image faded from the screen and the old wave of guilt swept over Thalia. She was one of the physicians who'd been so fascinated by Jennie's cold that they'd made no attempt to get her on the ship returning to Earth. Thalia had become Jennie's personal physician after that. And when she moved into her present administrative position, she had kept Jennie as her patient. She felt personally responsible.

Jennie Geiss was the only nonessential—that is, technically unskilled—person on Pythia. Thalia had tried to help her find things to do that would keep her from feeling useless, but the fifth-wheel syndrome was hard to combat. In the last few years Jennie had become increasingly subject to depression. Thalia had seen that she received therapy, of course, and that had helped. But it hadn't solved Jennie's problem.

Thalia had once talked to Jennie about implanting electrodes in her cerebellum that would let her turn off depression manually whenever she felt it beginning. But Jennie had resisted the suggestion stubbornly—and unreasonably, it seemed to Thalia. When asked why, Jennie had muttered something about wanting to keep her brain virginal.

Jennie's depressions had begun about the time Thalia first noticed that Pythian society was becoming stratified—a phenomenon that had not been present in the early days of the colony. She wondered if there was any connection between Jennie's state of mind and the newly rigid class divisions. Thalia thought this shouldn't have made any difference: Jennie, belonging to no one group, had a social mobility not enjoyed by any other person on Pythia. But perhaps it just increased her sense of rootlessness.

The scientists formed the aristocracy of Pythia, of course; and as in any aristocracy, there were ranks within ranks. But the scientists ran Pythia, and were responsible for the well-being of everyone on the planet.

Next most valuable were the experimental humans—people like Sam Flaherty of the webbed hands and feet. Or the cloned families. Or the ones with lungs that worked underwater. These people were watched over and cared for as if they were worth their weight in gold. Which they were.

Before the appearance of the animal workers, a third social class had formed the peasantry: the technicians—highly skilled men and women without whom Pythia simply could not function. But they were replaceable, as scientific geniuses and experimental humans were not. This alone set them apart.

Pythia was mostly machine-run, but the colony couldn't dispense with human services altogether. The air-recycling units, the automatic waste converters, the maintenance and repair machinery all needed overseers. Pythia also needed nurses and animal handlers. And people like Adelbert the Pharmacist.

On Earth, of course, class distinctions manifested themselves in outwardly visible forms—the ruling classes dressed better, ate better, owned more. None of this was true on Pythia. Everyone's physical needs were taken care of equally and automatically; the question of possession of property simply didn't apply to life on Pythia.

But caste-awareness did apply. No matter how carefully the experimental humans were instructed by the tutors who oversaw their education, the youngsters tended to look down on the technicians. Even the normals shared something of this attitude; they too were necessary to the outcome of whatever experiment they were controlling. The technicians, quite naturally, resented this.

And where did Jennie Geiss belong in this hierarchy of necessaries? Nowhere. She was not animal nor technician nor experimental human nor scientist. She was a leftover normal who happened to catch a cold at the wrong time. There were other normals on Pythia, members of control groups as Jennie once had been. But they were all children or adolescents, the oldest of whom were to be sent to Earth on the next ship. Jennie was, literally, in a class by herself.

Thalia Boyd roused herself from her musings. She'd never get off her answer to Earth's inquiry at this rate.

> *The widespread interest in transplants was directly responsible for solving one of Pythia's early problems. Attempts had been made to teach chimps whose intelligence had been raised to operate some of the machinery on the planet. But there were difficulties. Even though the chimps could understand what was*

expected of them, they couldn't always handle the equipment. The chimpanzee hand simply is not as dexterous as the human hand; apes in their natural environment use no tools harder to handle than twigs for digging, stones for cracking nuts, and leaves for grooming. So, as a logical next step, human hands were transplanted to the chimps.

And that had been the *other* experiment that had made chimpanzees into computer repairmen.

The hands came from cadavers provided by Earth for the organ bank Pythia maintains. The successful transplant of human hands to chimps led to further experiments—a dalmatian with webbed hind feet, a rhinoceros with an eagle's eyes, an otter with a dorsal fin. One of the more delicate operations was performed on a bear: he was given human vocal cords. The bear learned to approximate human speech sounds, but he could never talk in the normal sense of the word. He still had a bear's brain, a bear's mouth structure, and a bear's vision—which meant that he did most of his learning through scent. But he did learn to tell his handlers if he was sick or injured.

The bear had died last year, making the sound "urr, urr" over and over again. One of the bear's handlers had told Thalia that that was the animal's approximation of "hurt."

The ultimate goal of all chimera experiments is to discover new ways in which the human body can be augmented without having to resort to prosthetics. Transplanted animal kidneys, for instance, are vastly superior to implanted artificial kidneys, in spite of the artificial kidney's obvious advantage: no disease.

But an artificial kidney is still a machine, and like all machines, it needs to be serviced. Pythia scientists agree that repeated surgery, no matter how minor,

> *just can't be good for the body. So until a totally self-*
> *repairing machine can be perfected, transplanted*
> *animal organs will continue to be preferred.*

—And wouldn't Richard the Lion-Hearted have loved *that*, thought Thalia.

"Anything spectacular being done to Dan, or can I go in and see him?"

The attendant waved her on.

Jennie Geiss stepped on the escalator and rode to the third level of the building where the observation platform was located. She stood looking down at the complicated assemblage of wires, human organs, and electronic parts that was Dan. As always, she stared a moment at the human brain at the center of it all, and then moved to the nearest microphone.

She didn't say anything, waiting for one of Dan's roving eyes to become aware of her. Dan didn't like surprises.

It took about ten seconds for one of Dan's monitors to pick her up. The speaker in the wall behind her boomed into life.

"Jennifer, love, have you heard the news? They're giving me a spleen."

"A spleen? Whatever for?"

"For aesthetic balance, I suspect. Somebody probably noticed an empty space among all the wires and gewgaws and thought, 'Wouldn't a spleen look nice in there!'"

Jennie mulled it over. "I don't think that's such a good idea. No, I don't think that's a good idea at all."

" 'And why not?' he asked innocently."

"Didn't the ancients believe the spleen was the source of capriciousness in the human character? If you get any more capricious, Dr. Tirsos is going to demote you to an adding machine."

"Never. I made that man what he is today. He comes here every day at sundown and bumps his head on the floor three times in front of my number-two monitor."

"And when is the happy event to take place?"

"Which happy event? I have so many."

"When you get your spleen."

"A holy day was deemed most suitable. Michaelmas."

"Micklemuss?"

"September twenty-ninth to you, infant. If you'll promise to stop eating chocolate, I'll arrange for you to come in and watch. Perhaps you can—Ouch! That hurts!"

A young technician hurriedly removed his foot from an insulated wire he had stepped on and glanced uncertainly at the nearest monitor. "You're putting me on, aren't you?" he said.

Jennie recognized him. The technician had been a member of a control group, a normal who had later been trained in cybernetics for this particular job. He was still new at it.

"Putting you on?" Dan huffed. "Young man, I never. Put. People. On. Now kindly keep an eye on those gunboats of yours before you send me into anaphylactic shock."

"Yessir," the technician mumbled, backing toward the door.

"Why?" Dan asked plaintively. "What god have I offended? Never in the history of cyborgerdom have so many bucket-footed machine-nurses appeared in one place at the same time! And you, young man, are merely the latest pestilence sent to plague me! Fungus, begone!"

The technician fled.

Jennie laughed, and then said, "Kind of hard on him, weren't you? You know he wasn't hurting you."

"You know it and I know it, but until *he* learns what harms me and what doesn't, he's going to have to watch his step. Figuratively and literally. Besides, a man can get killed in here. He'll be more careful next time."

Dan meant well: two deaths had resulted from work on him, and both technicians had died because of their own negligence.

"You want something," Dan accused.

"Right. No, wrong. I came to tell you something."

"You're writing your next book about me!"

"Not the whole book. One chapter."

"One chapter? *One chapter!*"

"One chapter is all Dr. Tirsos is getting, and Dr. Tirsos . . ."

"Dr. Tirsos invented me?"

"Well, yes."

"Ah, but does he have any *chic*? Does his sparkling personality enliven the microfilmed page? Who's going to sell your book for you, Jennie me love—Dr. Tirsos or me?"

Jennie sighed.

"You must admit I have a point," Dan went on. "Have you written your Tirsosian chapter yet?"

"Rough draft. In longhand."

"Read it to me tomorrow, and I'll pass objective judgment on its salability."

"Objective judgment? You?"

"I am more capable of objectivity than any mere total human on this planet." Dan sounded slightly miffed. "Bring the chapter tomorrow. Do you hear me?"

"How can I help but hear you? The speaker's right behind me."

"Then bring it."

"Yes, *sir*!"

"Don't be smart. You know I made dozens of useful suggestions on your last book."

"Yes, you did," she admitted. "And I even used one of them."

"Out! *Out*! OUT!"

"You'll be sorry when I'm gone," she laughed.

She heard one final grumble—"One chapter!"—as the door closed behind her.

Dan was the pulse beat of Pythia.

He was the colony's repairman, detective, librarian, dispatcher. He controlled the energy sources that every instrument on the planet drew upon. If a thurascope in one of the operating rooms needed a new part, Dan signaled a technician in the area to take care of it. If a communicator radiated a weak signal, Dan strengthened it. If a garbage converter didn't convert, Dan would figure out why and then either fix it himself or yell for help.

At first Dan's function had been to control communications only. Originally he was one of three cyborgs deemed essential to realizing the full experimental possibilities that Pythia's scientists envisaged. (A machine that reproduced exactly all the parts of the human brain would have been larger than the entire planet.) The first cyborg, a patient soul named Georgia, was to serve as guinea pig for all the new medical treatments the Hippocratic *Wunderkinder* could think up. All vital organs of the human body had been added to Georgia, in one place or another, several times over; and radical surgery was performed on her almost weekly. But something had gone wrong. One bit of surgery proved to be *too* radical, and the oxygen supply system had picked that moment to malfunction; and before the damage could be repaired, Georgia was dead.

Then Dan became the guinea pig, but this time a more effective protective measure was added. No matter how many experiments were being conducted, one complete life-support system was never touched. A dozen experiments could fail simultaneously and be shut down without any harm resulting to Dan.

The third cyborg had been an uncommunicative fellow named Feodor who was used as the colony's power source control. But Feodor had never been able to adjust to being a cyborg. He steadily grew more and more withdrawn until one day he had quietly programmed malfunctions to all his vital parts. Suicide among cyborgs was not unknown, of course, but the entire Pythian colony had been deeply shaken by Feodor's act.

Pythia had had to switch to its emergency power system, which maintained enough services to sustain life until the main source of energy could be made operational again. All of Feodor's systems were transferred to Dan, and it quickly became apparent Pythia needed only one cyborg to fill all its needs. And Dan had the job.

He loved it.

Dan could never be accused of underestimating his own importance. Who else could carry on a hundred conversations simultaneously? Who else knew every fact that was known to man? Who else could talk back to Dr. Tirsos?

Dan was good at recommending books for leisure reading as well as providing vital information. Dan was hooked into all the computers on the planet and had often interrupted Jennie's book dictation to question her word choice. Dan stood guard over the weather control systems, the food-processing center, the clothing-recycling division, the educational machines, the sanitary facilities. He made suggestions, corrected errors, introduced improvements, and insisted on inserting his metaphoric nose into every phase of Pythian life. Dan could sometimes be a pain in the ass.

But he was a necessary pain. He did his jobs, and he did them well. His idiosyncrasies were good-naturedly tolerated, because nobody could ever quite forget Feodor.

Near Dan's building was a park which supplemented the let-off-steam rooms that were available in every structure on Pythia. Jennie waved to Claude Billings, who was energetically punching away at a dummy, and stretched out in a hammock to enjoy the artificial sunlight.

Just one more year.

Two nurses were taking turns throwing darts at a target to which they had pasted the photograph of one of Pythia's neurosurgeons. Must have given them a hard time in the O.R.

—One more year of this, thought Jennie, and I can go home.

Home. She had never been to Earth, and yet it was home. Pythia could never be home to the Jennie Geisses who were stranded there.

Two experimental children scampered by, their skin shimmering from blue to green as Jennie watched. In addition to being eye-pleasing, those two would never contract skin cancer. The children stopped to talk to Claude; he was part of the team that was experimenting with pigmentation.

Jennie didn't know a lot of the experimentals; but those she did know, she knew quite well. Eight years before, after she had caught her cold, she'd had to face up to the fact that she would have to find something to do with herself until the next ship arrived in nine years. Earlier testing had proved that Jennie had no scientific aptitude whatsoever, and her grasp of mathematics was so uncertain that she could never be trained as a technician. Jennie turned out to be a nonscientist adrift in a scientific community.

It was Thalia Boyd who had first suggested that Jennie consider teaching. Teaching on Pythia was accomplished by a machine–tutor cooperation that for the most part worked quite well. The machines took care of dispensing facts; but when value judgment was called for, especially in nonscientific areas, human tutors (mostly child psychologists) were needed as guides. Once Jennie had indicated her willingness to give it a try, the psychologists had quickly nosed out those of their students who had shown a special interest in nonscientific subjects and had sent them to Jennie. It was an ideal solution except for one thing.

Jennie was a lousy teacher.

After a year of what was perhaps overearnest endeavor on Jennie's part, she had settled into a pattern that didn't seem to cause too much damage. Only those students who showed an exceptional attraction to the humanities were sent to her, and this made her job do-able. Sometimes she even enjoyed it. Now she never had more than a few students to tutor at a time, but, even so, problems sometimes occurred.

Her two brightest students were Siamese twins named Edward and Matthew, who had not been separated until they were ten years old. Eddie and Matt couldn't add two and two, even helping each other. So they had decided that they would write plays. By the time they were fourteen, they were reading Ben Jonson.

"In *The Alchemist*," Eddie, the talkative one, had once said, "this character Dapper. Why does he put vinegar up his nose?"

"Part of his preparation to meet the Fairy Queen, isn't it?"

"Yes, I know, but why vinegar?"

"Well, why does he do any of the things he does? What's going on?"

"These other two guys, Subtle and Face, they're gulling him. They feed him this line of bull about meeting 'The Queen of Fairie' and he doesn't have any more sense than to believe them. So he gets all gussied up for the meeting—and puts vinegar up his nose."

"Which is just another way of showing what a fool he is. He literally vinegars his senses."

"I wonder what it feels like," Eddie mused. "I think I'll try it."

"You'll do no such thing!" Jennie was appalled. "An astringent like vinegar on that delicate membrane in the nose? It must be terribly painful." And she'd made Eddie promise her not to put vinegar up his nose.

What she hadn't known was that Matt was silently planning to do that very thing. And did it. His nose became inflamed to the point that he needed medical care, Eddie rolled on the floor with laughter, and Jennie's stock as a teacher dropped to near-zero.

So when Jennie had first mentioned to Thalia Boyd that she'd like to try to write a book about Pythia, Thalia had greeted the idea with enthusiasm. She'd even arranged for Jennie to have use of one of the computer rooms for two hours each day. Jennie doubted that she could have written her two books without the aid of the computer. It had proved invaluable in helping her translate scientific data she didn't fully understand into accurate layman's language. And Dan, with all his buttinsky ways, had, indeed, helped too.

Jennie rocked gently in her hammock and was on the verge of drifting off to sleep when she saw a disconsolate chimpanzee shuffling in her direction.

"Jacob?"

The chimp looked toward her. It *was* Jacob.

"You look as if you've lost your last friend. What's the matter?"

Jacob reached for his stylus and slate. *Toothache,* he wrote.

"Oh, you do have your troubles! Are you on your way to see your dentist? What time's your appointment?"

2:30.

"Then you have time for a glass of wine at the Omph. Would you like that?"

Jacob's lips stretched back in a grin that almost touched his ears. His head bobbed up and down.

"Well, let's go then."

The Omph was Pythia's one watering spot. Its official name was Pythia Community Center; but in the colony's first year someone had sardonically suggested it should be called Omphalos, "the navel of the world." "The Omph" it had been ever since.

Jennie and Jacob took their wine and sat at a small table. Seven or eight experimental humans were sitting around one of the larger tables, laughing and talking together easily. A young woman whom Jennie knew only as one of Dr. Tirsos's assistants came in. After looking around, she walked over to the experimentals and tried to join them. She was told there was no room. She hesitated a moment, and then left.

Immediately after that in came Sam Flaherty, the aquajock. He headed straight for the experimentals. There was room for him.

Jacob picked up the wine bottle with his human hand and poured Jennie and himself a fresh glass. An attractive couple came in, a picture-book couple—she, small and blond; he, tall and dark. Jennie felt her throat tighten: the man was Barry Gomez.

Jennie noticed absently that Jacob had filled her glass too full. If she tried to pick it up, the wine would spill.

Barry and the blond girl were sitting at the other side of the room, but it wasn't long until they spotted Jennie. Barry bent his head toward his companion, and then rose and approached Jennie and Jacob.

"How are you, Jennie?"

"The same. As you see."

"Mind if I sit?" And he sat. "Still with the red wine, I see."

"Any objection?"

"What right do I have to object? You make your own decisions, you told me so. A hundred times."

Jacob hastily scribbled *dentist* on his slate, thrust the slate under Barry's nose, patted Jennie's shoulder, and was gone.

"Was that an example of simian diplomacy?" smiled Barry.

"Only partially. He really does have a toothache."

A silence grew between them. Barry took a deep breath

and broke it. "Jennie, I want you to know I plan to move in with Cynthia Howell."

Jennie glanced over at the blond girl who was purposefully not looking in their direction.

"Why did you feel you had to tell me?"

He looked embarrassed. "I didn't want you to find out from someone else."

"Barry, you're a free agent," said Jennie. "You and I went our separate ways over three months ago."

"I thought you might be hurt if I didn't tell you."

"No, you owe me no explanations. Look. We had nearly two years together. I think that's a pretty good track record for both of us."

He didn't like that. "I just thought you should know," he said coolly.

"Well. Now I know."

He nodded his head and stood up abruptly. He walked over to Cynthia, touched her arm, and they left.

Jennie sat staring at the table where the two had been sitting. She lifted her glass in a toast, spilling wine over her hand.

"To Cynthia," she said aloud. "Long may she revel!"

Adelbert worked at tidying up a dispensary that had never been untidy.

—What are you trying to do? he asked himself. Prove you are of more value than a machine?

It was a futile hope, and Bert knew it. Mechanically he went about his self-appointed tasks—everything in its place, everything just so. As if anyone would notice.

Perhaps it would be better to go back on the next ship— better than staying on Pythia and contributing to his own obsolescence. The next ship would be carrying equipment that could do everything Bert and the other pharmacists did and more. He had been asked to remain on Pythia and oversee the new automated medicine dispensers which, Bert had no doubt, would work perfectly. He knew nothing about machinery; he was being kept as insurance against machine failure.

Once Pythia had tested the equipment and found it

satisfactory, Earth would follow suit. The best Bert could hope for back on Earth would be a job in some small community that lacked the wherewithal to automate his function. For all practical purposes, pharmacy was already a dead profession.

Bert checked his appearance in the mirror and nodded good-bye to his replacement. One of the Briles clone had agreed to meet him at the Omph for dinner—a real stroke of luck, since the experimentals usually treated him as if he were a piece of the furniture. The one he had made the date with was called Sharon; he wondered if they would play a trick on him and send one of her sisters in her place. Since all eight of the girls were identical, he wouldn't know he'd been tricked unless he was told. But Bert wouldn't mind. Just so *somebody* showed up.

At the Omph, he ordered a cocktail and wondered whether Sharon-or-whoever would listen while he tried to talk his way to a decision. Bert had not yet reached his thirty-fifth birthday. If he stayed on for one more tour of duty, he'd be forty-four by the time he left for Earth. Too old to learn a new profession. And too disappointed to try. He'd had a good nine years on Pythia. But.

An hour later he ordered a cheese sandwich to go and went home.

Thalia Boyd took out her dead husband's picture and inspected it closely.

Yes. That was what he'd looked like.

She put the picture away, wondering how it was possible to miss someone *that much* and not always be able to remember his face.

A reminder light flashed on the control panel. "Aliotto hearing, Dr. Boyd," a voice boomed out. "Conference Room C, ten minutes."

"Thank you, Dan," said Thalia. Of that she *didn't* need to be reminded.

Outside the conference room she met Dr. Tirsos. "Thank you for coming," she said. "I'm afraid this is going to be a sticky one."

"Has he no explanation at all?"

"Not that I know of. We'll have to see."

The others were already inside, seated around the conference table. Two men, two women. Dr. Indhara, the tall, elderly Asian who had gone into research in spite of his natural surgeon's hands. Dr. Aliotto, a large man with a slightly accusing look on his face—which was interesting, since he was the accused.

Dr. Angelina Baker was a large black woman in her late forties. The look on *her* face was impatient, even a little bit angry. The fourth person at the table was Cynthia Howell— very young, very pretty, and very scared.

Thalia Boyd and Dr. Tirsos took their places. "I have asked Dr. Tirsos to be here in an advisory capacity," she said to Dr. Aliotto. "Do you have any objection?"

"No."

"Very well, then. Dr. Indhara, will you state your charge?"

Dr. Indhara focussed his eyes on some neutral spot on the wall and began to speak. "Dr. Aliotto neglected to exercise proper control of the incubation of the new culture medium we have developed," he stated flatly. "The medium requires a gradated five-step increase until an exact, optimum temperature is reached. Last Thursday a batch of the medium had been taken through the first four steps, and Dr. Aliotto left the laboratory without increasing the temperature for the final gradation."

"What is the new culture medium for?" interjected Dr. Tirsos.

"For growing staph antibodies. Dr. Boyd has our reports. I take it you've not read them?"

"No."

"Well, as you know, staph is the most persistent antigen we've ever had to deal with; it's able to develop a resistance to just about anything, given enough time. It has the capacity to lie dormant, encapsulated, until we're fooled into thinking we've got it licked. Then it surfaces again, more virulent than ever. That's why even now we never have a completely clean O.R."

—We don't really need the lecture, thought Thalia. Aloud, she said, "Dr. Indhara, why was the incubation Dr.

Aliotto's responsibility? That's usually the lab assistant's job."

"Because of the extraordinary nature of this particular antibody. It's an especially precious one, one I didn't care to entrust to any but the actual research directors themselves. We have at last developed a strain that we are sure staph will not be able to build up a resistance to. We've been testing it in the laboratory for eleven years, and *not once* has any variety of staph been able to fight off the new antibody."

"Not even dormant staph?" asked Dr. Tirsos.

"Not even dormant staph. We exposed the staph briefly to the antibody—just enough to 'inoculate' them. Then we allowed the staph to go dormant. When the inoculated or 'experienced' staph reemerged, we once again exposed them to the antibody. The staph collapsed immediately."

Dr. Tirsos grunted his surprise. Thalia knew what he was feeling; they had all long ago accepted as fact that staph could not be destroyed. The most they had ever hoped for was maximum containment.

"Are you ready to try it on Dan?"

"We are. Or at least we were until the lab assistants— fortunately—caught Dr. Aliotto's failure to increase the temperature of the culture medium. If the error had not been detected, we would have gone ahead and used the medium, which, of course, would have been inadequate as a nutrient source for the antibody. The result would have been a weakened antibody, incapable of destroying the staph we were planning to insert into Dan's specially constructed circulatory system. If Dr. Aliotto's carelessness had not been discovered, Dan would probably be dead right now."

"Surely not, Doctor," said Dr. Tirsos. "Remember, Dan has a supplemental life-system that's never used in experimentation."

Dr. Indhara chose his next words carefully. "The staph we were planning to use on Dan is so virulent that without the new antibody it is virtually uncontrollable. With only the weakened antibody to fight it, we'd lose control immediately and the staph would spread like wildfire. And this means that in all probability *all* of Dan's life-systems would be infected."

Silence.

"I'm sure," ventured Thalia, "you have some checking system that would prevent such a disaster."

"Of course," said Dr. Indhara. "That's why we're here right now."

Another silence.

"Who found the error?" asked Thalia.

Dr. Indhara nodded toward the girl. "Cynthia."

"Cynthia, how did you discover the last temperature increase had been omitted?"

"Part of my routine, Dr. Boyd," the girl said. "On this particular project Dr. Indhara assigned all the lab assistants to triple-check every stage of the incubation. I check on Dr. Aliotto, Don Silver checks on me, and Shen Te-sun checks on Don. Only when all four of us have signed the incubation checklist is any particular stage considered complete."

"Do you have the checklist with you?"

"I have it," said Dr. Indhara, producing a sheet of paper from his briefcase.

Thalia glanced over the paper quickly and handed it to Dr. Tirsos.

"There are four signatures under each culture medium listing up to number J-19—dated last Thursday."

"It was the J-19 batch that wasn't increased," said Cynthia hurriedly. "I couldn't sign it because Dr. Aliotto hadn't signed."

"So what did you do when you saw Dr. Aliotto's signature was missing?"

"Well, first I checked the temperature gauge and saw it was still on its stage-four setting, and then I looked at the list and saw Dr. Aliotto hadn't signed. So I asked Don about it—Don Silver, the lab assistant who checks on me—and we agreed that the time that had elapsed since Dr. Aliotto was supposed to increase the temperature was probably too great for the medium to be salvaged."

"How soon after Dr. Aliotto increases the temperature do you check the gauge?"

"About half an hour."

"Go on."

"So we called Dr. Indhara. He looked at the gauge and the

checklist, and ordered batch J-19 destroyed."

"And was it destroyed?"

"Yes. Immediately. Don and I took care of it ourselves."

"Dr. Aliotto," said Thalia, "is there any part of the statements made by Dr. Indhara or Cynthia Howell that you wish to challenge?"

"No."

"Then you don't deny the accuracy of the accusation that is being made against you?"

"No, except to say it isn't the whole story."

"What *is* the whole story? Why didn't you increase the temperature of batch J-19?"

"I left early on Thursday. I had a personal matter to attend to, something not connected with the lab in any way. Around noon I left a note for Dr. Baker asking her to take care of the J-19 increase for me at five P.M. precisely."

Thalia looked at the black woman.

"He did leave me a note," said Angelina Baker. "And here it is." She slid a piece of paper across the table to Thalia.

Thalia read the note, and it said just what Dr. Aliotto claimed. "Well? What happened?"

"What I didn't know," Dr. Aliotto said, "was that Dr. Baker wasn't in the lab that day. She didn't get the note until Friday morning."

—Oh, Jesus Christ, thought Thalia. "Why didn't you just leave a message with Dan? He would have notified *somebody*. And didn't you check back to make sure Dr. Baker had received your note?"

"Evidently not. It must have slipped my mind. I really don't know."

—*It must have slipped my mind*. Dan could have been destroyed, and all Aliotto could come up with was 'It must have slipped my mind.'

"Let me add something," Angelina Baker said. "It's easy to see how this happened. I've got a couple of transplants coming up that I want to use the antibody for. So I've formed the habit of going to the lab to learn everything I can about it. And I want to say Dr. Aliotto has been an absolute godsend. His help has been truly invaluable."

Thalia nodded, not too impressed. That was part of his job.

"Anyway, I've been in the lab almost every day. Last Thursday was the first day I'd missed in—oh, almost a month, I'd say. Naturally Dr. Aliotto thought I'd be there. It was a natural assumption to make."

No one seemed to have anything more to add, so Thalia asked the four to leave while she consulted with Dr. Tirsos. Then Dr. Aliotto was called back in.

"Dr. Aliotto," Thalia said, "you are hereby relieved of your duties. You will return to Earth on the next ship, and you will engage in no more research nor in any medical activity of any kind during the remainder of your stay on Pythia."

"Now, wait a minute!" Dr. Aliotto's voice rose. "I endangered no lives! I ruined one batch of culture medium, that's all. There's no way in which that culture could have been used to grow the antibody—not with three other people checking after me. That's the whole purpose of the checking system, to keep errors from becoming fatal. I made a mistake, yes. But it wasn't that serious a mistake!"

"I disagree," Thalia said, and Dr. Tirsos nodded. "The primary thing that keeps Pythia free from the senseless waste of life common to so many Earth hospitals is our refusal to tolerate the kind of casualness toward one's work that you displayed last Thursday."

"So I'm to be an object lesson?"

"Not at all. None is needed. You are being relieved of your duty not to warn others, but because you have demonstrated you are unreliable."

"*One* mistake! One *small* mistake!"

"A mistake that can't be minimized. You *were* responsible for increasing the temperature of J-19 at five o'clock on Thursday and you did not do it. Nor did you make adequate arrangements to have it done for you. If it hadn't been for Dr. Indhara's foresight in instituting a threefold checking system, Dan could have been destroyed. And there is no one at Pythia—I repeat, *no one*—who is as important to our survival as Dan is. Anyone who poses even a minimal threat to Dan is a threat to all of us. And you are accountable for your actions, just as every one of us on this planet is."

Thalia paused for a moment. "Dr. Aliotto, I can't tell you how sorry I am this has happened. But surely you understand that Pythia *must* uphold a policy of accountability—if we are to survive."

Dr. Aliotto's face had been darkening steadily. "How dare you speak to me like that!" he burst out. "I'm not a child, to be lectured to in this way!"

"For that I apologize. I know you're not a child."

"I want you to know I don't accept this. I don't accept it for one moment. If you think I'm going to go quietly back to Earth hat-in-hand begging for a job, you're sadly mistaken. I can't do anything about it now, because you're in charge here. But when I get back, I'm going to demand an inquiry. I'm not going to let it rest here."

"That is your right, of course."

"You're damned right it is. And you'd better have a good explanation for wasting a year of my life." And he stormed out.

Thalia let out the breath she'd been holding, and Dr. Tirsos patted her hand. "You did the right thing, my dear. Don't let him upset you."

"It's an upsetting situation."

"Give him some time to cool down. He tends to speak rashly on occasion."

"I'll give him all the time he wants."

Angelina Baker stuck her head through the door and said Thalia's name. "I'm just going," said Dr. Tirsos, and left the two women alone.

The black woman came straight to the point. "Honey, you made a mistake."

"Oh, Angelina, don't *you* start. The man's careless."

"He's also a damned good worker and I need him."

Thalia stared at her friend in surprise. "And that's reason enough to wink at ineptitude?"

"It's reason enough for me. Besides, he's not really inept. I want him back. Doesn't that count for anything? It was a dumb thing to do, granted. But that's not enough reason to kick him out."

Thalia sighed. "There are mistakes and there are mistakes.

Errors in judgment are understandable when they're committed while exploring unknown areas, where we have no guidelines to help us. But *slovenliness* is a whole different ball game. I've seen it happen too many times before—shrugging off one casual error as unimportant, then another, and then another. The time to stop all that is after the *first* error. Aliotto's just too big a risk. I'm sorry."

Angelina shook her head. "I sure hope you know what you're doing."

"Which means you don't think that I do," Thalia said wryly. "Do you think I enjoy this sort of thing?"

Angelina suddenly grinned. "No, I don't think you do. And I deserve a big kick in the ass for telling you how to do your job. I still want him back, but I'm not going to bug you about it."

For such small favors Thalia was grateful.

"How was it?" Barry Gomez asked.

"Awful," Cynthia said. "I stood outside in the hall and listened to him shouting at Dr. Boyd."

"Did she shout back?"

"No, she never shouts. She just quietly kills you."

"Oh, come on, Cyn."

"Well, she didn't have to relieve him of his duty altogether, did she? She could just have taken him off the project...put him to work on something else. Or maybe...maybe just suspended him for a few weeks."

Barry laughed. "You talk about Thalia Boyd as if she were a schoolteacher—slapping wrists and saying 'Naughty, naughty!' She has an *enormous* responsibility, Cynthia; keeping Pythia functioning efficiently isn't exactly a breeze, you know. It was a simple preventive action she took—that's all."

"You think she's right?"

"Yes, I do."

Cynthia's lower lip was trembling. "I just wish *I* hadn't been the one."

Barry saw she was seriously disturbed; he put his arms

around her and pulled her close. "So that's it," he said softly. "Feeling guilty. But what else could you do? Increase the temperature for him, sign the sheet, and pretend nothing had happened? You know you couldn't do that. You'd be endangering Dan."

"I know," she said in a muffled voice.

"So stop blaming yourself. You had no choice."

She burrowed her head against his chest. "I just wish it hadn't been me."

Dr. Indhara sat in his quarters waiting for his wife. The female Dr. Indhara was an oral surgeon; she and her husband had come to Pythia seventeen years earlier, and neither of them had ever regretted the move.

Sitting in semidarkness, Dr. Indhara was feeling relief more than triumph. He admitted for the first time how worried he'd been that Thalia Boyd might not take Aliotto's error seriously enough. There had been the very real possibility that Thalia would simply reprimand Aliotto and transfer him to another project. So few people truly understood the importance of *every* detail in a discipline. Thalia Boyd, fortunately, was one of them.

He was experiencing a curious emotional letdown. It's times like this, he thought, that I could do with the consolation of a philosophy. But he had none. The masturbatory quality of Buddhism had always distressed him—holding spiritual intercourse with one's self.

The door slid open. His wife took one look at him and knew something was wrong.

"She let him off," she said.

"No." Dr. Indhara rose and kissed his wife lightly.

"Then what?"

"I'm not sure, Maya. It's just occurred to me to question my own motives. I've never really liked Aliotto. Perhaps there was a little *Schadenfreude* in my quickness to report him." He shook his head. "I don't know, perhaps I'm getting old."

Maya Indhara smiled at her husband. They had both been

old for quite some time. Her tone was gently mocking as she asked, "You mean to say you wouldn't have reported him if you liked him?"

"Of course not!" He looked shocked, and then realized she was teasing him. "There's no doubt in my mind that Aliotto is too casual about his work. What's doubtful is my own personal pleasure in seeing him found out."

Maya laughed at him outright. "Even with effective staph antibodies, my dear, you can't have *everything* antiseptically clean. Oh yes, I know it would be more comfortable if reporting Dr. Aliotto were totally free of any complicating human response on your part. But since that's not the case, well then, you'll just have to live with that terrible raging guilt of yours."

This time they both laughed. Dr. Indhara stretched his arms high over his head and began to relax. What man needed a philosophy when he had a Maya to put things into perspective for him?

Dr. Joseph Aliotto was not feeling guilty. He was angry— more angry than he had ever been in his life, and he was making very little effort to hide the fact.

"Come on, Joe, ease off," Angelina Baker said as he tossed down his third scotch. She had talked him into coming to the Omph for a drink, but now she was beginning to think it wasn't such a good idea.

He poured himself another without answering. Adelbert came in and waved to them self-consciously as he looked for a table. The word was out, then.

"Has this ever happened before, Angelina?" Aliotto asked. "Has anyone at Pythia ever before been kicked out?"

The black woman shrugged. "Not that I know of. You've been here as long as I have." Eight years.

"That bitch. I could kill her."

"Thalia Boyd's no bitch. And you know it."

"Hey, I thought you were my friend."

"I am. But I'm Thalia's friend too. Look, don't make a personal thing out of it. You'll get your chance to appeal."

"A year from now. What the hell am I supposed to *do* for a year? Twiddle my thumbs?"

Angelina had no real answer to that. "Well, one thing you shouldn't do is nurse your resentment. We've all got to live together until the ship arrives."

"Oh, Christ, save me from platitudes! That's the last thing in the world I need right now, Angelina. I know you're trying to help, but I think the best thing would be for me to go off by myself for a while. The way I feel now, I just might bust somebody's jaw. And I'd rather it not be yours."

"Me too," she said, startled. She watched him lumber his way out of the Omph, broadcasting hostility as he went.

If only she'd gone to the lab that day, she could have prevented all this! *That* day, of all days. That was the day she had stayed away deliberately because she had just realized *why* she'd been going every day. Not because of the staph antibody. Because of Joseph Aliotto.

There she was—a middle-aged woman with two husbands behind her, with a bad case of the hots for an Italian pathologist. Joe was impulsive and a little hot-headed—not the best qualities to be found in a research scientist. And not the best qualities for making friends. Angelina had heard no one call him by his given name; that was one reason she had made a point of calling him Joe as soon as she comfortably could. The other reason was that he was attractive, *her* kind of attractive. Attractive enough to make her ask Thalia Boyd to reconsider her judgment even though they both knew carelessness was Pythia's number one enemy. And Joe Aliotto had been careless. Angelina was vaguely disturbed that her attraction to the man had even momentarily obscured her responsibility as a scientist.

She reached for the bottle of scotch and found that Aliotto had taken it with him.

Jennie Geiss shuffled her papers aimlessly, and then, in a fit of pique, swept them all to the floor. Very dramatic. Now pick them up.

Exercise: one, two, three, and four. One, two, three, and four. One, two, two-and-a-half, quit.

Paint pictures: daub, daub. No yellow. No black. No talent.

Take a bath: splash.

Work on the book: Now is the time for all good men.

Yell: aaarrrrrrggggh!

Screw.

Jennie punched out Claude Billings's number and the audioscreen wavered into life.

Claude's sleepy face peered out at her. "Jen?"

"I woke you up."

"Naw, I just got in. Skin transplant ran into trouble."

"The one you're trying on Dan?"

"That's the one. Dan's not the most patient patient I've ever worked with."

"Did he give you a hard time?"

"No, not really. When he saw we were having trouble, he shut up."

"Claude. Come over tonight."

That opened his eyes. "Sure, Jen. What time?"

"Not before nine."

"I'll be there."

Jennie shivered slightly and Claude pulled the bedcover up over her shoulder. They were always so solicitous at first.

Claude was a good lover, and Jennie felt comfortable with him. They were lying spoon position, with Claude's hand on her stomach. After a while life returned, and Jennie poured them some wine. They lay completely relaxed, sipping the wine and talking.

"Jen, what happened to you and Barry?"

"I really don't know," she said absently.

"Don't want to talk about it?"

"No, nothing like that. I really *don't* know." She held some wine on her tongue for a moment before she went on. "We seemed to bring out each other's hostilities. It finally got to the point where we were both angry all the time. Not especially angry at each other—just angry."

"He certainly was angry when you broke up."

They both laughed easily. Barry was a weather controller; and on the day he moved out of Jennie's quarters, he had gone straight to the weather-control station and treated Pythia to a Grade-A, Number-One snowstorm. In summer.

Jennie put the snowstorm out of her mind and snuggled closer to her new lover. He felt good. Nevertheless, some of the warmth had gone out of the moment. Claude's asking about Barry was a *gaucherie* she could have done without.

Claude kissed her ear and rubbed his cheek against hers. She knew they were both wondering about the same thing: what would it be like to live together? Claude might be just what she needed—nice, pleasant, uncomplicated Claude.

Oh, well. No hurry.

Jennie needed music. She pressed the button that connected her with the computer's record library. One of the old tenors, she thought. She checked the listings and punched out the code for Beniamino Gigli. What selection? Something sad and romantic. She chose Monteverdi's *Lasciatemi morire*.

(Here you are, folks, the Green Mountain Boys singing "They Shot Me in My Rear, Hey!" From *La Fanciulla del West*. Or perhaps *Der Freischütz*.)

One minute and forty-eight seconds later Jennie hit the replay button. The only thing wrong with *Lasciatemi morire* was that it was too short.

When she hit the replay a second time, Dan's voice cut in on her. "Enough of that sad stuff, love. Mustn't feed a depression. How about *eine kleine* Mozart?" And the upbeat, life-affirming notes of one of the airs from *Figaro* filled the room.

Jennie listened for almost a minute before she shut it off.

It had been a mistake to tell the twins to read the romantic poets.

Eddie had been going on for ten minutes about the glories of a nature he had never seen. He extolled the virtues of "the

natural life" (Earth) as opposed to those of "the artificial life"
(Pythia). It was clearly a case of adolescent rebellion finding
its target.

Finally Jennie had had enough. When Eddie started
rhapsodizing about regenerative cycles, she said simply,
"Bullshit."

That temporarily stopped the flow of words.

"What?" he said in an astonished voice.

"You heard me. *Bull*shit. You're going off the deep end
with this thing. You're making nature into something totally
warm and comforting and benevolent."

"You telling me it isn't?"

"I'm telling you nature can be destructive too—or had you
forgotten that little fact?"

"But *basically* it's good."

"What do you mean by 'basically'? It's in the nature of
nature to be destructive as well as regenerative. Ever since
Wordsworth invented nature, those who speak with
admiration of the naturalness of a thing ignore fully fifty
percent of what they admire. Natural bodily processes would
have killed most of us off years ago if we hadn't interfered
with nature. It's unfortunate that the word artificial has
acquired such an unfavorable connotation. But civilization
itself is built upon artifice. Nature not only can be but ought
to be improved upon. The natural way is not automatically
the best way; sometimes it's the worst way possible. And I'm
not talking about natural disasters like tidal waves and
hurricanes."

"Example?"

"Well. On Earth, the land is dry. The farmer despairs of
ever harvesting his crop. A cloud floats over and releases
rain. Crop saved. Good or bad?"

"Good, of course."

"The land is saturated from heavy rains. Seed is rotting in
the ground, farmer despairs. Same cloud floats over and
releases more rain. Good or bad?"

"Oh, now you're stacking the deck."

"Not me. Nature. Do you think a cloud drops rain on dry
land because the land *needs* it? Does nature provide us with
what we require because it is in sympathy with our efforts to

survive? Believe me, Eddie, nature couldn't care less."

"I never said nature intended anything, one way or the other. But the absence of good intentions doesn't mean a thing can't be inherently good."

"Nature *is* inherently good. But it is also inherently destructive. It's not an either/or question. Nature is both good and bad, everywhere, all the time. And artifice is our way of converting bad into good."

"So ultimately nature will be *made* to be all good?"

"If our artificial means are strong enough, yes. If you want something positive to believe in, believe in *that*. But understand that good and bad are merely human interpretations that nature itself doesn't recognize. Years ago Dylan Thomas wrote, 'The force that through the green fuse drives the flower drives my green age; that blasts the roots of trees is my destroyer.' Same force. Different results."

"Why did he say 'green fuse' instead of 'stem'?"

"Extra syllable. Sense of impending explosion. I don't know, I'm not a poet. The point is, don't romanticize nature. It's life-sustaining and essential, and it's life-destroying and needs to be controlled. Repressed. *Contained*. Artificially."

Eddie was trying hard to look convinced but wasn't quite succeeding. Jennie sighed and dismissed her student.

She wasn't cut out to be a teacher.

A week after lecturing Eddie on the nature of nature (the meaning of meaning?), Jennie considered calling Thalia Boyd. Her latest bout of depression had lasted far too long. Although Thalia had recently changed Jennie's medication, the new tranquillizer didn't seem to do any more than the old. About the only times Jennie felt alive any more were during her bed sessions with Claude. And as soon as he left, the depression returned.

She wasn't sleeping. At nights the most she could hope for was to drift into a few moments of semiconsciousness, usually followed by a leadenness for an hour or, at the most, two. She became nervous and irritable.

She had begun to cry easily and often. A careless word, an unintentional snub, a short answer, the casual cruelty of other insecure souls in search of ego boost—almost anything was enough to make her withdraw into herself even more during the day. At home in her own living quarters, all the slights, real or imagined, would come pouring out in crying jags that would last a couple of hours.

All movement seemed to require concentrated effort. Get dressed. Trousers. Bra. Tunic. Now move. First this foot. Now that. Lift your hand. Press the button. Now what? Everything took so much *effort*. Some mornings she hadn't been using her computer time because she couldn't bring herself to get out of bed.

In less than a year she would be making her long-delayed voyage to Earth. But try as she would, she couldn't generate any real enthusiasm at the prospect. There were no guarantees that life on Earth would be any more fulfilling than on Pythia. She had forced herself to make plans: she would spend a month learning her way around New York City (was a month long enough?) and then she would travel. Then she would write *A Pythian's First Impressions of Earth*. That was her publisher's idea. Since Jennie hadn't been able to come up with an alternative, she'd go along with it.

What a yawn.

She moved lethargically around her quarters, picking things up and putting them down again. Abruptly she turned to the control panel in the wall and tried to call Thalia Boyd. Not in. She sat down in a chair by the window and stared at the mountain peak in the distance.

An hour and a half later she was still sitting there.

The machine projected the printed words upon Jennie's bedroom wall; she was reading a rather stilted early Elizabethan play about Beowulf.

Hro.   Beowulf, be ruled
    By me: face not this monster unattended.
    My lords and I bear arms against him nightly,
    And proudly follow your command.

Beo.   Hrothgar,
   'Tis unseemly I repel your proffer'd aid;
   But when two beasts do struggle for dominion,
   Savage law doth isolate those two,
   Whilst others, watchful, keep their safe remove.
   Brute law rules this land: the brutalness
   Of Grendel must I measure 'gainst my own.

Hro. As you will.

Beo.   Know this, Hrothgar: 'tis
   Grendel draws me here, not Heorot.
   My half-completed soul long has waited
   For that one moment in eternity
   When my enemy and I, face to face,
   Should know each other. Though that juncture be
   But one mere speck upon the face of time,
   I would not share that speck with any man.

Hro. A glorious moment, truly.

Beo.   Seal glory
   In a jar; it soon evaporates.
   'Tis knowing that's the prize: to see unclothed
   The horror and the doubt we've dared not look on,
   The testing that is yet to come, the present
   Falling out of balance—all in one
   Outside of one, detached, and visible.
   Young warriors early learn to arm themselves
   With knowledge of the enemy. How smoothly
   Slides the phrase! But yet how rough and rare
   The bringing-off. Fighting only shadows
   Is an exercise for madmen. Hrothgar,
   I would see your Grendel.

    And so would we all, thought Jennie, so would we all. But
he doesn't exist.
    That would be too easy.

• • •

Jennie decided not to ask Claude to move in with her.

Thalia Boyd studied the test results attached to the proposal for a new experiment.

A team of the younger scientists had developed a substitute for luciferin, a substance found in light-emitting organisms such as certain clams, jellyfish, and fireflies. By itself, luciferin would remain stable when heated. But when combined with oxygen and the enzyme luciferase, it would be destroyed by an oxidative reaction that gave out light. As part of a tracing system in the human blood stream, it would be invaluable. Unfortunately, luciferin turned out to be rather hard to pin down. Not a single compound common to all luminous organisms, luciferin existed in many different forms—just as there were many different vitamins.

The research scientists who had developed pseudoluciferin, the substitute substance, were proposing that it be used specifically to detect the presence of the kind of melanoma that shows no clinical signs (such as a change in skin color). It had already been tried out on Dan, and the test results were positive. The research team was now requesting permission to test it on human subjects.

Thalia was displeased. She thought the idea of an artificial luciferin was a good one and that such a substance probably could be perfected. What displeased her was the fact that the young scientists had anticipated so very little in the way of pitfalls. They *assumed* that light emission had no significance to the organism possessing bioluminescent ability (never proved). They *assumed* that the amount of energy liberated through molecule excitation would remain small even when an artificial substance like pseudoluciferin was involved (not known). They *assumed* the continuing oxidative breakdown of an artificial substance within the bloodstream would have no detrimental effect on the cell wall (not tested).

Also, there wasn't a single mycologist on the research team. Those luminous mushrooms that grew in a circle (the

glowing "fairy ring" of medieval legend) were semitoxic—
that is, they were poisonous to some people though others
could eat them with no ill effects. Could it possibly be the
luciferin in the mushrooms that produced this unpredictable
reaction? And if so, couldn't pseudoluciferin also affect
different people differently? In short, there was no evidence
that pseudoluciferin would not destroy some lives while
saving others.

Thalia activated the recorder and began to dictate
specifics of the new tests she wanted conducted.

Barry Gomez looked down at Cynthia Howell, who was
sleeping peacefully in his arms, one hand curled up like a
baby's. Such a pretty child. Such a child.

He punched the code for a soundless light show that
sometimes provided him with a moment's needed distrac-
tion; but this time the changing patterns on the wall failed to
hold his interest.

What was wrong? Cynthia never gave him a hard time, or
made unreasonable demands, or let whim dictate the quality
or frequency of their love-making. Sometimes Barry longed
for a good old-fashioned scrap with Jennie.

No. Mustn't think that way. Comparisons are odorous, as
Jennie used to quote somebody named Dogberry as saying.
Jennie. It always came back to Jennie.

Damn the woman.

He watched a blue amoeba-shape swallow a fireball and
turn purple. Life with Jennie had not been happy, but life
with Cynthia was banal. (Odorous, odorous!) Barry wasn't
convinced a happy life must be a placid one, but his own life
was no proof to the contrary. Irritated, he switched off the
light show and crawled in beside Cynthia, his movement not
disturbing her. God, how he wished he could sleep like that.

Suddenly he was angry, very angry—at Jennie. Jennie,
with her neuroses, constantly making simple things complex.
That useless woman had taken up nearly two years of his
life—and for what? For nothing. He should have kept it a
casual affair. He'd been stupid to let her get to him like that.

In sudden appreciation of the prize he had, he nuzzled the neck of the girl next to him.

Cynthia slept on.

"What's going to happen to Dr. Aliotto?" Jennie asked. "What's he going to do until the next ship arrives?"

"Take a long vacation," Thalia answered.

"I think he'd like to work on Dan. Claude says he was asking about the possibility."

"Dr. Tirsos doesn't want him anywhere near Dan."

"Couldn't you just *assign* him to Dan?"

"I could, but I won't. Not without Dr. Tirsos's approval. Dan's his baby, you know that. What is this, Jennie? A one-woman lobby for Dr. Aliotto?"

"No, I barely know the man. I was just wondering what he was going to *do*."

"He doesn't have to do anything, you know. He's been relieved of his duty."

"He'll want to do something. He can't just sit on his hands until the next ship. Everyone has to have something to *do*."

Thalia looked at her closely, and then said, "Are you feeling depressed again, Jennie?"

Michaelmas.

"Jennifer, my love, isn't this exciting?"

Jennie peered down at the knot of people clustered about the area where Dan's new spleen was being installed.

"I can't see anything," she complained.

"Just as well, just as well. There should be some mystery left in life, don't you think?"

"No, I *don't* think."

"That is merely *one* of your problems. Ah—careful there, boys."

"What do you mean, 'boys'?" growled a woman's voice.

"Sorry, Dr. Baker," said Dan blandly. "I forgot you were there."

"Like hell you forgot. Now shut up and let me concentrate."

"Of course, dear Doctor, of course." Dan held his silence for almost fifteen seconds. "Jennifer, I have been thinking over your chapter on Dr. Tirsos, and I have decided it's really very well done."

"That probably means it needs more work."

"My, my! Aren't we all tetchy this morning! What *is* the matter with you people? Too many positive ions in the atmosphere?"

"Shut up," Angelina said.

"Perhaps someone should check on the weather controllers," Dan went on. "Jennifer. That young man you were so besotted with for a while. Larry?"

"Barry," Jennie said, annoyed.

"Ah, yes. Barry. Barry the Weather Man. Why don't you—Dr. Baker, you have the delicate touch of a sledge hammer."

"Right now I wish I had a sledge hammer."

"I'm leaving," Jennie announced.

"That's right," Dan said petulantly. "Desert me in my hour of need."

"Uh . . . Jennie, isn't it?" asked Dr. Aliotto.

"That's right. Jennie Geiss. I've come to ask a favor. I need help on my book. The computer can help me only so far, and I've reached that point. Since you, er, have some free time now, I thought you might be willing to help."

Dr. Aliotto's mouth smiled while the rest of his face remained immobile. "Did Thalia Boyd put you up to this?"

"Thalia knows nothing about it. It's my idea. I need help," Jennie persisted.

Dr. Aliotto looked her straight in the eye for a full minute before answering. "So you thought you would provide useful work for the disgraced citizen, is that it? I thank you for your concern, but it's out of the question."

"Dr. Aliotto—"

"I am a research scientist!" he exploded. "Not a writer of pop literature for the semiliterate!"

Jennie stared at him in astonishment.

"Up yours," she said, and walked out.

• • •

"I don't want to."

"Jesus Christ, Jen! You never want to any more. What's the matter?"

"Nothing's the matter, Claude. I'm tired. I don't know."

"You're always tired. Or depressed. Or something. Do you want me to leave?"

Jennie rubbed her temples. "No, Claude, I don't want you to leave."

"Then what? You never want to make love any more."

"You said that."

"And I'm going to keep on saying it until I get an answer."

"I don't have an answer! Get off my back, will you? I feel as if I'm going to explode!"

"Why?"

"*I don't know why*!"

Claude couldn't think of anything to say. He put his arms around her, and she leaned her head against his chest. In another minute or two they would both start saying they were sorry.

"Jennie, a word with you, please." Dr. Tirsos led her back into the computer cubicle and closed the door. "I hear you asked Dr. Aliotto to help you with your book."

"How did you—" Jennie caught her tongue between her teeth. "He must be talking about it. I never said a word."

"It was a very generous gesture on your part, but a misplaced one, I'm afraid. I've always suspected Aliotto of having a nasty streak, and now I'm sure of it."

"Perhaps it was too soon after the hearing," Jennie suggested. "Perhaps after he's had time to cool down and think it over...."

"Then he can come to you. You've made your offer; don't press him. He's short-tempered, Jennie. Better just leave him alone."

Jennie saw the concern in the old man's eyes and decided to pay attention.

"All right," she said.

• • •

"Hi, Sam," Jennie said.

Sam Flaherty flapped past, pretending not to see her.

"Jennie, how many times do I have to tell you? You've already used up this month's prescription."

"Come on, Bert. Just five grains."

"Not even one grain. Not until the first of next month."

"Only five grains. Nobody will miss it."

"That's not the point. I can't give it to you."

"Adelbert, don't be such a stick."

"You know I'm supposed to report you for this. Stop asking me."

"So report me. But report me *after* you give me the stuff."

"*No*, Jennie! You've got a hell of a nerve putting me on the spot like this."

"Some friend you turned out to be."

"Friendship has nothing to do with it."

"Bert, I'm begging."

Bert picked her up bodily, kicked the button that activated the dispensary door, and deposited her firmly outside in the hallway.

"And don't come back until the first of next month," he said, wagging a chubby finger at her.

"Barry. What are you doing here?"

"'Lo, Jennie," He was propping himself up by her door, trying to look her in the eye. His pupils were jumping.

"What are you on? You're flying."

"Doing my best. Is Billings here?"

"Claude? No."

"Are you sure?"

"What do you mean, am I sure? Of course I'm sure."

"He might be sitting in a corner someplace where you overlooked him."

Jennie didn't answer that, not certain where the conversation was heading.

"He's a little bland for your tastes, isn't he, Jennie? Billings is the only guy I know who can enter a room and make you think two people just left. But maybe you just like variety."

Jennie counted to ten and asked, "Why did you come here, Barry?"

"Just feeling a little affluctionate. How about it? Got anybody in bed right now?"

She closed the door in his face.

"Whassamatta, Teach?" Eddie asked, while his twin, Matt, looked at her reproachfully. "You don't like our *parvum opus*?"

"I'm sorry. I don't seem to be able to concentrate."

Eddie gave an exaggerated sigh while Matt started pulling at his ear. "Maybe she doesn't like blank verse," the latter suggested.

"I love blank verse," said Jennie absently.

"You just don't like *our* blank verse," said Matt.

"What?" Jennie forced her attention back to the twins.

"My name is Eddie," the first twin said seriously, "and this is my brother Matt. We're your students. Remember? And we have just placed in your hands Act I of a brand new original Shakespe*her*ean play, writ by hand. The lamentable tragedy of King Henry the Tooth. The play you've been encouraging us to write. The play you couldn't *wait* to read."

"Perhaps I'd better read it later," Jennie said guiltily.

"Perhaps you'd better," said Eddie and Matt.

"Jacob, I need a friendly listener."

Headache, wrote the chimp on his slate.

"Some other time," said Jennie.

Thalia Boyd was feeling every one of her forty-three years, and admitted it.

"I don't know what it is, Jennie," she said, stirring her coffee. "There's something happening every minute. Picayune things. Things that have never happened before, and nobody seems able to handle them. I'm exhausted."

"What kind of things?"

"Well, this morning two of the men working at the animal compound actually got into a fist fight. It seems they couldn't agree which one of them was supposed to feed the wolves."

"Did they want to feed them or *not* to feed them?"

"They wanted not to. They both claimed they had more work than they could handle. Quite a few people have begun making that same complaint these past few weeks. The same sort of work they've been doing for the past eight years. But now, all at once, it's too much."

A burst of raucous laughter made both women look up. A table in the corner of the Omph was occupied by half a dozen experimental humans who seemed to be demanding the attention of the others present.

"Yesterday one of the disposal machines broke down," Thalia went on. "The one that directly services Dan."

"Oh, wow."

"Yes. I could hear him complaining before I even entered the building. He had his volume turned up to full and was keeping it there until the machine was repaired."

"Dan's never been very patient."

"No. But my point is that things like this—a work schedule dispute, a mechanical breakdown—these are not problems that ordinarily demand special attention. There's a corrective and repair system built into every facet of Pythian life. Why did those men's supervisor send for me? I did nothing he couldn't have done himself in half the time. And when Dan's disposer broke down, why didn't someone just press the unit repair button? Nobody seems to be *thinking*."

"Couldn't Dan have initiated the repair himself?"

"Yes, he could have. When I asked him why he preferred hollering about the breakdown instead of doing something about it, he got huffy and said he didn't wish to discuss the matter."

"That's odd. What did Dr. Tirsos say?"

"Nothing. He was as surprised as I was."

Just then eight identical teenage girls appeared in the entrance to the Omph. Their laughing chatter broke off abruptly when they caught sight of Thalia Boyd. As one person they turned and left.

"What was that all about?" asked Jennie.

"The Briles family," said Thalia. "I cloned them myself, back before I took over the administrative duties of Pythia. I've always had a special interest in them, naturally. But for about a year now they've been going out of their way to avoid me. I don't know why."

While Thalia was talking, a soft bleating sound had begun. The two women looked at each other uncomprehendingly.

"What on earth is that?" asked Jennie.

"I have no idea. I've never heard it before."

Jennie watched as Thalia walked over to a control panel in the wall and punched out a number. She returned almost immediately.

"It seems that that peculiar noise is an alarm," she said. "A yellow alert has been called. I must go to the control center. Come along."

The buzz of excitement hit them the minute they opened the door to the control center. Small groups huddled together studying monitors as the soft bleat pulsed through the air. Thalia headed toward a tall, balding man seated before the main viewscreen.

"What is it, Charlie?"

The man she'd called Charlie glanced over his shoulder at her and turned back to the screen. "Glad you're here, Dr. Boyd. Take a look at this transmission from Uraniborg." Uraniborg, the planet named after Tycho Brahe's observatory, was Earth's furthermost outpost. "See that yellow dot? That's a ship."

"The supply ship? What's it doing near Uraniborg? It's not due for—"

"It's not the supply ship."

"What, then?"

"Don't know. It just appeared on Uraniborg's tracking screen."

"Is it headed for Pythia?"

"Could be. We'll know better in a few hours. We'll have more checkpoints to calculate from by then."

"Can you estimate its speed?"

"No, not accurately."

"Then you don't know when it would get here?"

"Not under a week, I'd say. But that's just a guess. I can tell you as soon as we're sure of its speed."

Thalia stood staring down at Charlie's bald spot. "Well," she said, "we can't have that sheep bleating over the loudspeaker system for a week. Somebody turn off the alarm."

The bleating stopped.

"Charlie," Thalia said, "what about the monitors circling the rest of the planet?"

Charlie pointed to a double row of screens picturing either water or unrelieved mountainous terrain. "All working," he said.

"How high can they go?"

"Two miles. They're not designed to transmit farther than that."

"So we have no way of getting a good look at this thing before it lands? If it lands."

" 'Fraid not. We can follow it in from two hundred miles, but how long a look that will give us depends on its speed."

"Can three or four of our monitors be redirected to observe the landing?"

"Easily. We don't need all those transmissions of water surface anyway."

Thalia nodded. "That's what we'll do, then. As soon as you've determined the ship's speed, get in touch with me. I'll notify Earth."

As they left, Jennie asked, "What if he—they—it—tries to land in the colony? By crashing through the shield or something?"

"The shield is supposed to be impenetrable." Thalia smiled wryly. "But I doubt that it's ever been tested against space ships."

By early the next morning they had a few more answers. The ship was definitely headed toward Pythia, and its speed indicated it would enter into orbit in thirty-six hours. "Fast bugger," said Thalia.

It didn't take long for word of the strange ship to spread,

and Thalia decided to make a public announcement. "There's no need to be afraid; we haven't been threatened," she told the eager and anxious Pythians. Half of them silently added "Yet." Only Dr. Tirsos seemed unconcerned.

"If it's going to land, it's going to land," he said. "No point in getting worked up until we know what's happening. We'll just have to wait and see."

"A space ship!" exclaimed Dan. "A real honest-to-god unidentified space ship! Marvelous! Oh, marvelous! I'll run a check on the monitors. I *must* see the landing!"

"Everybody will see it," said Jennie. "Thalia's ordering an all-channel relay once the ship reaches the two-mile limit."

"Thoughtful of her. Now you can all lie comfy in your beds and watch the arrival of the Monster from Outer Space."

"Ha. Nobody's going to be in bed when *that* ship lands."

"And you, I suppose, will be out there to greet him, strewing flowers in his path and offering him the keys to the city."

"I never strew. Besides, that's the bad part. Nobody can meet him. He'll have to land outside the shield."

"What about those clumsy-looking suits that can be worn outside?"

"That's not the problem. The problem is getting to wherever he lands. We have nothing but small surface transports, and you know what the terrain around us is like."

"Up and down, up and down."

"Mountains and crevasses, right. We don't even know if he'll come down on this landmass."

"Oh, he'll come down here, all right. Put yourself in his place, dollink. If you were orbiting a planet that was all water and mountains except for one rather large blue bubble plunked down in the middle of nowhere, what would you head for?"

"The blue bubble," they said together.

"He'll land near here, never you fear," Dan went on. "So you'd better have the red carpet drycleaned and break out the champagne. It's best not to antagonize Monsters from Outer Space."

"So my old mother always told me," grinned Jennie.

Dan sniffed. "You no more had a mother than I did," he said.

"Why would he be coming here?" Jennie asked Claude.

"Maybe we're the nearest landfall to his home planet."

"But he passed within tracking distance of Uraniborg."

"That's true, he did."

"And surely there'd be some kind of unmanned exploration first?"

"Maybe that's what this is. We don't know there are living creatures in it."

"Perhaps that's what they are—creatures."

"You mean with green scales and ten arms and antennae six feet long?" Claude laughed. "You've been talking to Dan, I'll bet."

Jennie smiled. "You know, I suspect he halfway hopes for something like that."

"He would. Do you think Dan's tastes are growing a little decadent?"

"No more than anybody else's. I think we could all do with a change."

Adelbert stood quietly, waiting for Dr. Baker to make up her mind.

"Sorry to cause all this trouble, Bert," she finally said. "I hope this will be the last change I'll have to make."

"No trouble," the pharmacist smiled. He liked the big, friendly black woman who occasionally shared a beer with him. His chubby fingers flew over the computer keyboard, locking in the new prescription she had just written out.

"What d'you think's in that space ship?" Angelina asked idly. It was the question everyone was asking.

"Machines," Bert answered promptly. Machines were always disrupters of the *status quo*. "Nobody would make a long flight without testing it out first with machines."

"Machines can carry bugs as well as people can." Angelina was worried about the quarantine measures Thalia Boyd had set out; she wasn't sure they were strong enough. "Just so nothing from the ship is brought inside the shield too soon. Until we're certain it's safe."

"Maybe it won't land."

"That would be best for us."

"You mean you don't want to know what's inside?"

"Well-l-l," Angelina grinned, "I didn't say that."

They were watching a group of adolescent experimentals and normals who were laughing and singing—and thoroughly obstructing the main thoroughfare.

"Look at them," said Thalia. "Those two groups haven't been that friendly since they were children. What do they think they're doing?"

"They're preparing a welcome for the alien," said Jennie.

"A welcome? We don't know what's on that ship, and they're preparing a *welcome*? Good god in heaven, do they think this is a game? And look at that sign—Greetings to the Monster from Outer Space!"

"That's Dan's influence, I'm afraid. He enjoys playing guru every once in a while."

"Well, they'll probably party themselves out before the ship enters its orbit. Let's hope so, anyway."

Cynthia Howell was becoming fidgety, Dr. Indhara noticed. She always tugged at the neckline of her lab coat when she was nervous.

All the lab workers were a bit on the edgy side. Only half their mind was on their work, he knew; the other half was out in space with the alien ship. Well, he wouldn't hold them long; they'd just clean the equipment from this last experiment and call it quits for the day. He was as curious as any of them.

The tinkle of breaking glass caught his attention. Cynthia had dropped a tray of slides she had just removed from the sterilizer. Without saying anything she grabbed the manual vacuum and squatted down. Dr. Indhara was startled to see she wore no underclothing.

He stood and watched as she fumbled with the starter on the vacuum. He did not tell her to hurry.

A laugh drifted in from the next room just before the vacuum hummed to life: it was his wife's laugh. Had she told him she'd pick him up today? In a few seconds Maya would be in here and see Cynthia—like that.

"That's good enough, Cynthia," he said. "The maintenance machines will get the rest."

Cynthia stood up just as Maya Indhara walked through the door.

"What's all this?" asked Jennie. "Are you going to try to make voice contact?"

"Yes," answered Thalia. "Charlie thinks it may be possible."

The control center was quiet, abnormally quiet. The party in the street had long since ended; most work had slowed down or stopped altogether.

"If we can establish any kind of communication, we may be able to direct it to our own landing area." Everyone else had quickly developed the habit of saying 'he' and 'him'; Thalia deliberately said 'it,' referring to the ship itself rather than to any possible occupant.

"Then what?"

"Then, if there's no overt act of hositility, we put on our suits and go out to investigate." Thalia's suit was on a table beside her, ready. "If it comes down somewhere in the mountains, then we'll just have to wait some more."

"Let him come to us?"

"If possible."

"Here he comes," said Charlie.

All eyes strained toward the viewers. A flash filled the screens and then immediately receded. The screens were blank.

"What's wrong?" asked Thalia.

"Our monitors can't follow him," said Charlie. "He's going too fast."

"He'll have to slow down to orbit. Redirect the monitors to pick him up when he does. Got anything?" This to the communications engineer.

"Audio disturbance," the engineer said. "He's got some sort of communications system, but he's not using it."

"That answers one question, anyway," said Thalia. "There wouldn't be a communications system on board unless there was someone there to use it."

Silence.

"Number sixteen monitor!" a voice shouted.

Number sixteen was tracking the slowing ship. Gradually a shape emerged on the screen. An asymmetrical sphere with what looked like a landing base.

"Get the other monitors on him," said Thalia. (It was no longer possible to say 'it.')

"They're already on their way," answered Charlie.

They watched as one by one the other monitors zeroed in on the ship. Now it was visible from all angles. The ship seemed to be inspecting Pythia's terrain.

"He's over our landmass now," said Charlie. "Look! He went past the landing area close enough to spot it. Now he's adjusting his orbit. He'll set down next time around."

Charlie was right. The ship eased around the planet's curvature and angled gently until it was parallel to the surface of the landing area. Then, with a minimum of fuss, the ship was down.

"It'll take him some time to conduct tests—" Thalia began.

"Like hell," interrupted Charlie. "Either I'm seeing things, or that's a landing ramp."

It was a landing ramp, and it quickly connected the sphere with the planet's surface.

"Don't open the shield until I tell you," Thalia said, grabbing her suit and running out. Jennie hesitated, torn between her curiosity about who or what the screen would show coming down the ramp and her desire to be on the spot. She decided to go with Thalia.

On the way to the only entrance built into the shield, Jennie soon lost sight of Thalia. Curious Pythians were swarming toward the entrance; others were bunched in front of the exterior viewscreens.

Charlie's voice rose above the crowd's murmur. "It's a man. At least he has human shape." Jennie glanced at a screen to see a tall humanoid figure step off the ramp onto the planet's surface. "He's not wearing a protective suit," Charlie continued, surprised. "How can he—look! He's heading straight for the entrance!"

"Don't open the shield," cut in Thalia's voice.

"Shield remains closed. Dr. Boyd?"

"I'm almost there. Get another monitor on him, can you? I want a better look."

"How's that?"

"I still can't see him clearly."

Jennie pushed her way through the crowd. She caught a glimpse of Thalia by a wall control panel ahead.

"He's at the entrance! Should I—"

"*Do not open the shield*," Thalia said. "Do not let him in until I've had a chance to make contact."

Then came Charlie's voice, strange: "It doesn't matter. He's inside. He broke the shield. He's inside."

The crowd quieted, became motionless. The screens showed only the empty exterior of the shield.

"How could he be inside?" Thalia asked, unbelieving.

"I don't know. But he's inside."

No one moved. Then Thalia started walking, alone, carrying her now unneeded suit. Eight steps. Ten steps. Then she stopped.

He was there.

A communal intake of breath is an impressive thing, but by nature less impressive than the phenomenon that prompts it. All other feelings—curiosity, uneasiness, perhaps outright fear in a few cases—were overridden in an instant by that unique shock occasioned only by exposure to absolute beauty. That perfect thing of beauty—so rare that awareness of the possibility of such perfection is itself a gift—now was offered to the gaze of the Pythians.

The alien was not so much a man as he was a picture of what man thought he should be. Larger than the Pythians, perfectly proportioned, kingly. Golden hair, a golden shimmer to the skin, golden pupils. Motion in repose.

Strength. More than strength: power.

A realized ideal.

The stranger stood quietly, watching them, waiting. Several minutes passed, with no threatening gesture made by either side. Thalia seemed as if struck dumb, unable to move. Jennie edged up beside her.

"Thalia?"

No answer.

Jennie looked at the stranger. His eyes met hers, neither defying nor appealing. She felt a brief stab of panic when she thought she read invitation there. You must come to me, the golden eyes seemed to say.

She hesitated a moment, and then stepped forward— hand out, palm up.

The stranger smiled.

Part II

Dionysus.

> *Like it or not, this city must learn its lesson:*
> *it lacks initiation in my mysteries;*
>
> . . . .
>
> *... And when my worship is established here,*
> *and all is well, then I shall go my way*
> *and be revealed to other men in other lands.*

> —*Euripides*
> The Bacchae

"Whoo-*ee*! what an entrance!" Eddie said. "When he stepped up and took your hand, I felt as if my brain had started sprouting feathers. Weren't you scared?"

"Yes," Jennie admitted.

"What are they doing now?"

"They're trying to work out some form of communication. The alien seems to prefer learning our language to trying to teach us his own. At least, that's Dr. Boyd's impression."

Jennie thought Thalia's attitude toward the stranger rather odd. Once it was clear that the outsider intended no harm and had come in friendship, most of the Pythians welcomed him warmly. Including Dr. Tirsos. But Thalia had held back. It was her job, of course, to make dispassionate judgments, but surely a small gesture of *bienvenue* would not have been out of place. Thalia was obviously suspicious of the stranger.

"Do they know where he's from?" Matt asked.

"No. They showed him the astrographic catalogs, and after he'd studied them, he just laughed and shrugged. Either he couldn't read them or his star system hasn't been charted yet. The language problem is going to have to be solved first; then we can get some answers."

The problem lasted a week. Pythia maintained several tutorial machines programmed to teach English as a foreign language for the benefit of those scientists who had not spoken English on Earth. The use of the machines two hours daily usually produced proficiency in the language within a month or six weeks. The alien ruined one of the machines the first day; he ran it nonstop at full capacity for twelve hours before the overloaded circuits finally gave way. But by the end of the seventh day, the alien could talk to the Pythians.

• • •

"My name is Zalmox. My planet is called Nisa by its inhabitants, Kret or Frija by others."

"What others?" Thalia Boyd demanded.

One golden eyebrow rose slightly. "Inhabitants of other planets," Zalmox answered reasonably. "Our . . . neighbors, one might say."

"These neighbors. Are there many of them?"

"Billions. Upon thousands of planets."

"And you've visited them all, I suppose."

Zalmox smiled. "Not yet."

Not yet. Thalia thought she detected a slightly patronizing tone in the alien's voice, which might or might not be attributable to the fact that he was speaking a foreign language. She suspected he was laughing at her—not at her personally, but at her as the representative of a race of beings who presumed to think they were unique in the universe.

"We would welcome all the information you can give us about these other races, and your own. We've been trying to make contact with sentient beings on other planets for many years now, but so far we've had little success. We know there's life in the Epsilon Eridani system—but beyond that, nothing." Thalia hated justifying *Homo sapiens* to this smiling intruder, but natural caution warned her to go carefully. "You must realize what a big moment this is for us—something we've been dreaming about literally for centuries has at last come true." *And we still don't know whether it's a good dream or a nightmare.* "But there is one thing I must know before we go any further. How did you breach our environmental shield?"

The alien didn't answer immediately, and when he did it was clear he was choosing his words just as carefully as Thalia had chosen hers. "Forgive me, Dr. Boyd, but I feel I can't tell you that just now. Later, perhaps, when we trust each other more. But right now you are suspicious of me— yes, you are, and it's perfectly natural that you should be. You don't know me, you don't know what I might do. But look at it from my point of view. I don't know you either— and I don't know what *you* might do. How I got through your shield will have to remain my secret—because I might need to get through it again. To get out."

Checkmate.

All right, try a different approach. Thalia touched a button on the control panel at her elbow. A screen at the end of the conference table lit up; projected on it was a three-dimensional image of one of the star charts Pythian technicians had drawn from the computer on board Zalmox's ship. Thalia experienced a moment of disorientation looking at the strange configuration. "The green knob on the panel at your right hand controls a pointer on the screen. Show me your planet."

The alien fiddled with the pointer control until he got the feel of it. A bright dot of light moved across the screen until it reached a perfect circle slightly left of center. "This is Nisa." The light moved. "This is our star." The light moved again. "And this is Tmol, the only other planet in our star system that sustains life."

"Colonized?"

"No. Life developed independently on Nisa and Tmol, but not simultaneously. Nisa's is the older culture."

Thalia stared at the chart glumly. "This doesn't mean much to me. Where is Nisa in relationship to, well, some astronomical signpost we know?"

"How do you change the projection?"

"Red button."

Zalmox bypassed several charts until he came to the one he wanted. "There. Familiar?"

Thalia studied the chart and shook her head. "It wouldn't be, unless it had been drawn up from our perspective. What am I looking at?"

"I think you call the constellation the Archer."

"Sagittarius?"

Zalmox nodded. "I don't believe your astronomers have charted that part of the galaxy yet?"

"No, it isn't visible from Earth. Where is Nisa?"

The pointer light moved. "My star system is in this cluster, here, enclosed by this triangle. You can see our position in relation to Sagittarius."

"Dead center of the galaxy, it seems."

"What a strange phrase," Zalmox smiled. "But yes, that's right. Dead center."

Thalia sat looking at the chart in silence. He *could* be telling the truth. The dust clouds at the center of the galaxy made visual observation from Earth impossible. Even the superobservatory on Uraniborg couldn't penetrate the haze that lay in that direction. Thalia realized she was the first Earth person ever to see what lay behind those obfuscating clouds, the first to see a diagram of the very heart of the galaxy. A small thrill of excitement rose in her.

And quickly died away. There was no way either to prove or disprove Zalmox's story. But if one wished to disguise one's point of origin, what better way than to claim home lay in a part of the galaxy still shrouded in mystery?

But why would he lie, what would he have to gain? Was he a scout for some invasion-minded race that didn't want its base of operations known? Was he—*Oh, stop it!* Thalia told herself sharply. This was mere melodramatics.

An oversweet aroma from the alien roused her. "What do you call your star?"

"Dya."

What to ask next. *Is all "human" life based on the carbon cycle; what kind of government do you have; where are all these other life-supporting planets; do you wage war; does Nisa have a plentiful supply of molybdenum; how is your ship powered; how technologically advanced is life on other planets?*

"Why have you come here, Zalmox?"

The alien was quick to catch undertones. "Meaning do I pose a threat to your community? No, my purposes are peaceful. I'm an agronomist. I carry in my ship a supply of fruit trees that I plant wherever I find fertile soil."

A celestial Johnny Appleseed? "You spend your time planet-hopping, looking for new orchard land?" Thalia couldn't keep the disbelief from her voice.

"That's right," Zalmox smiled. "The tree I carry bears a fruit that has medicinal as well as nutritional value. It is life-enhancing as well as a treat for the palate. I would like permission to plant some of my stock inside Pythia's artificial environment."

• • •

"So, Jennie, we are to believe that our mysterious visitor has come to Pythia for no purpose other than to cure our ills."

"Beware of monsters from outer space bearing gifts, Thalia?"

"Something like that. To be sure, he does claim his ultimate goal is to set up some kind of reciprocal agreement in which we would grow the fruit and he would act as distributor. When I pointed out that we were not a farming community but a colony established to conduct medical research, he was quick to answer that even more than others we should be interested in his fruit."

"What's it supposed to do?"

"It's supposed to cure schizophrenia, no less. I suggested he meant 'relieve the symptoms' rather than 'cure.' But he thought back over his newly-acquired vocabulary and announced no, 'cure' was the word he wanted."

"You don't like him, do you?"

"I don't trust him. Well, look, Jennie. He appears out of nowhere and refuses to establish voice contact from his ship. He breaches our supposedly impenetrable shield and doesn't explain how. He just happens to come from a part of the galaxy we can't check up on. And he refuses to submit to a medical examination."

"Oh?"

"Afraid we'll hurt his pretty body, no doubt."

"That's not unreasonable, Thalia. He doesn't know us. For all he knows, he'd be putting his life in our hands."

"That's what Dr. Tirsos thinks, but *I* think it's fishy. No, our smiling friend isn't being completely open with us."

"Are you going to let him plant his fruit?"

"Yes. If the blasted stuff does have any medicinal value at all, we ought to know about it."

Zalmox spent hours every day answering questions and providing information about his astral travels. The information was transmitted both to Uraniborg and to

Earth, where astronomers were evidently in a seventh heaven of their own.

("Have you noticed," Thalia said to Dr. Tirsos, "how Zalmox manages to say very little of his own race?"

"Why, I thought he was being quite cooperative."

"He's cooperative enough when he's talking about races other than his own, in other star systems. But try pinning him down about Nisa—somehow the conversation always gets back to these other places. Had you noticed that?"

"No," admitted Dr. Tirsos, "I hadn't.")

The planets Zalmox had visited were in star systems unknown to Earth astronomers—with one exception: the largest of the three planets circling Tau Ceti. On Earth, computers began humming away, estimating the cost of a new network of radio relays.

One more part of the universe had opened up.

"How can you breathe this stuff?" Eddie asked from inside his suit.

"My respiratory system is different from yours," Zalmox answered. They were outside the shield, where a group of Pythia's technicians was going over the alien ship inch by inch. Zalmox was watching them carefully, to make sure they didn't dismantle something essential that they might have trouble putting back together again.

"I know your respiratory system is different," objected Eddie, "but how? Why don't you *die* out here? We would, without the suits."

Zalmox sighed. "Do you really want a full lecture on my respiratory processes accompanied by 3-D projections and a quiz when I'm finished?"

"I guess not," Eddie admitted.

"Don't you get scared?" Matt interrupted. "Out there in space, all alone?"

"It's not frightening."

"Isn't it lonely?"

"I don't find it so. I don't think you would either. I think you'd like it."

Both boys looked at him expectantly.

Zalmox laughed. "All right, I'll take you for a ride before I leave."

Eddie cheered; Matt nodded quietly, satisfied.

A technician peered out through the escape hatch of the alien ship. "Zalmox, could you give us a hand?"

Zalmox pulled himself into the ship; the twins pushed in after him. Six Pythian technicians were inside; one was saying something about the extraordinary amount of unused space in the ship.

The technician who'd called Zalmox had to turn up the volume of his suit speaker in order to be heard over the twins' *wow*s and *gee*s. "How do you remove this housing, Zalmox?" He pointed to a seamless module of a piece with one of the bulkheads.

"Why, I really can't say," answered the alien. "I've never had any need to remove it."

"What's inside?"

"One of the booster drive's autorepair units." Zalmox pressed a series of keys on a control panel and a diagram appeared on the viewscreen. "That's what it looks like."

The technicians crowded around the screen. After a while one of them murmured, "Sure would like to get a look at the real thing."

"Sorry," smiled Zalmox. "Afraid I can't help you."

"Why didn't you answer from your ship when we first tried to establish voice contact?"

"I was having trouble with my communications equipment, Dr. Boyd."

"Were you."

"Why should I lie?" Zalmox smiled.

"This," Dr. Tirsos said, "is Dan."

"This" moved one of his monitoring eyes toward the alien on the observation platform. Zalmox stood motionless as the eye examined him carefully, moving up and down the tall body, taking its time.

"Genetically engineered," pronounced Dan.

A burst of laughter rang out from the platform. "Thank you, Dan," said Zalmox, still laughing. "That's quite a compliment."

"You mean you *aren't* genetically engineered?" Dan sounded peevish.

"Afraid not. Just a natural-grown product."

"Well, you're not at all what I'd come up with if I were designing a monster from outer space."

"Dan's little joke," said Dr. Tirsos hurriedly.

"What I mean is," Dan complained, "you aren't the least bit *menacing*-looking."

"Did you want me to be?"

"Frankly, yes. Look at it from my side, dear boy. I labor mightily at creating the proper atmosphere of fatalistic foreboding and old-fashioned goose-bumpery—and you show up all smiling and friendly and looking like a thespian sex symbol and spoil the whole thing."

"I didn't realize I was ruining your act," Zalmox said with a straight face. "I do apologize."

"Your apology is accepted," Dan said graciously. "Do you need an agent?"

"I think we'd better go," Dr. Tirsos said.

Zalmox said good-bye to Dan and followed Dr. Tirsos outside the building. The alien glanced at the doctor. "Something bothering you?"

Dr. Tirsos cleared his throat. "I know you must be sick of answering questions, Zalmox, but there's something that puzzles me."

The alien nodded.

Dr. Tirsos stopped walking, forcing his companion to do the same. "Why are you alone, Zalmox?"

"What do you mean?"

"I mean I could understand an exploratory crew's showing up here unannounced. Even a military operation of some sort would make a kind of sense. But one man, alone? Why take such risks?"

"The risks I take are minimal."

"Minimal! How do you know what you're going to run into when you land on a new planet?"

"I don't. It's one of the things that make my job interesting."

"But a few of these races you've described sound incredibly primitive, and primitive peoples invariably fear and hate what they don't understand. Yet you come hurtling through space to land on their planet and you say the risk is minimal? I'd think they'd kill you on sight."

"Actually, the primitive planets are the easiest. Most of the time the people take one look at me stepping out of my nice shiny space ship and decide I'm a god. Nothing helps business like instant deification."

"But the danger—"

"The danger is part of the job. As it turns out, I've always been made welcome, Dr. Tirsos. Every place I've been. *Every* place."

The alien's implication was clear: *Why should Pythia be any different?*

"Hello," said Zalmox, "you look familiar. What's your name?"

Jacob, scribbled the chimp.

"What if something went wrong with your ship in space?" Thalia asked. "Could you handle all the repairs yourself?"

"My ship is self-repairing," said Zalmox.

"No machine is totally self-repairing," Thalia stated flatly. "It seems to me you'd want to have at least one technician with you."

"Do you take a mechanic along every time you step on one of Pythia's moveways?"

"That's hardly a valid analogy—I can always step off a moveway."

"And I can step off my ship onto another, if the need should ever arise. I can always call for help."

"With your faulty communications system?"

Zalmox said nothing for a moment. Then: "Dr. Boyd, I travel alone because I prefer it that way. It's no more complicated than that. It gives me a freedom of movement I wouldn't have otherwise. Is that so hard to accept? That I value freedom of movement?"

"How very romantic," said Thalia dryly.

Bert dabbed at the perspiration on his forehead, wondering how he'd been dragged into this. "Two hundred meters, right." He fiddled with the multidialed timer board. "Just a minute."

Zalmox and Sam Flaherty stood poised at the edge of the pool. Curious Pythians crowded around, wondering how this little competition would turn out. They were of two minds. If there were anyone who could give Sam Flaherty his comeuppance, surely it would be this superendowed alien. Still, there was something about rooting for the home team . . .

Bert pressed the start buzzer.

Two simultaneous flashes of movement, and the race was on. A murmur of excitement rose from the onlookers as the water churned around the streaking racers. Zalmox and Sam were swimming in unison: smoothly, efficiently, with no waste motion. And *fast*. Silence fell as those watching began to realize what they were seeing. Never before had man moved so rapidly through water as Zalmox and Sam were moving now.

The two swimmers touched the end of the pool and made a simultaneous turn. Matching stroke for stroke they propelled their way back the length of the pool. When they made their second turn, Bert checked the timer and gasped.

How could arms and legs move that fast? Especially through water? Drag alone should make such speed impossible. And yet—and yet there they were, at the last turn, now starting their drive home.

Suddenly it no longer mattered who won the race, it didn't matter at all. Just the existence of such swimming, such superhuman effort—that was enough.

Bert crouched down to eye-level with the timer board so he could watch the dials and the swimmers at the same time.

A hand touched the pool endwall; a light flashed on the timer board.

Zalmox had won.

A dripping Sam Flaherty was coming toward him. "Time, Bert?" he gasped. "What's the time?"

"I—I—I don't believe this," stammered Bert. "Winning time, 0:58.93. Your time, Sam—0:59.02. You both swam two hundred meters in less than a minute!"

A great jungle cry of triumph rang out as Sam leaped high into the air. "I did it! I finally did it! I swam the two hundred in under a minute! Hey, Zalmox! Great race, *great* race! Congratulations!"

The air was suddenly filled with congratulations—for both Zalmox *and* Sam. When the hubbub had died down a little, Sam said to Bert, "You know, Bert, that was the greatest swim I ever had in my life. It was almost . . . effortless. As if I were being pulled along. I'd push against the water and feel it slip past me so easily—so smooth, so fast. It was great. Great."

Pythia had witnessed two miracles: Sam Flaherty had lost a race, and Sam Flaherty didn't mind.

"How long ago did you leave Nisa?" Thalia asked.

"This last time?" Zalmox thought back. "About two hundred years ago."

"*Two hundred years!* Did you say *years*? How old are you?"

"Weeks—I meant weeks. Two hundred weeks ago."

"Zalmox, you said 'years.'"

"I should have said 'weeks.' A mistake."

Yes, thought Thalia. *But what kind?*

"I know he's in there," Angelina Baker muttered.

Zalmox nodded and said nothing.

Angelina touched the door chime again. "Hey Joe! Come on, open up!"

When there was no answer, she turned to the alien. "I'm sorry about this, Zalmox. Truth is, I'm kind of worried about

him. He's been holed up in there ever since . . . ever since some
trouble a while back. I think he was the only one on Pythia
who didn't turn out to witness your rather spectacular
arrival. To be honest, that's why I asked you to come with
me. If curiosity about *you* doesn't bring him out of his shell,
nothing will. I hope you don't mind."

The alien smiled easily. "Of course not. I've acted this role
before, on other planets. I've a certain novelty value."

"Yeah, well, it isn't every day we get to meet a monster
from outer—*whoops*."

Zalmox laughed. "That's all right. I've met Dan."

Angelina turned back to the door with fresh determination. "Aliotto," she roared, "get your ass out here or I'll break
the fucking door down!" She grinned at Zalmox. "And I
could do it, too."

The door hissed open. A bleary-eyed, unshaven Aliotto
stared out at them with undisguised hostility. When he saw
the alien on his doorstep, his mouth dropped open and a
strangling sound came from his throat.

"Zalmox," Angelina announced, "this unspeakable mess
is Dr. Joseph Aliotto—pathologist, drunkard, and former
human being."

"It's the middle one that interests me," Zalmox said as he
pushed his way in past the open-mouthed Aliotto. "What
have you got to drink?"

Since their host seemed incapable of speech, Angelina
answered for him. "Probably some scotch around somewhere. Ever taste it?"

"No." Zalmox picked up a bottle from a table. "Is this it?"

"That's it. Hold on." Angelina hunted around until she
found some glasses. "Pour three."

The two visitors made themselves comfortable. Angelina
glanced at Dr. Aliotto, who was still standing by the door and
said, "You might as well sit down, Joe. You've been
invaded."

"Ah-h-h," murmured Zalmox, tasting his scotch.

Dr. Aliotto finally found his voice. "Where did you come
from?"

"From a backward planet that never learned to make
scotch. Will you give me the recipe?"

Dr. Aliotto looked startled. "I don't make it myself."

"Pity," sighed Zalmox, taking another swallow.

"Ahem," said Angelina. "How about some ice?"

"Ice machine's broken," Dr. Aliotto said absently. "What's your name? What did she call you?"

"She called me Zalmox. Which is my name."

Dr. Aliotto sank down into a chair and shook his head. "The last I heard, some sort of unidentified ship had been spotted. I was drinking at the time. I didn't even know you were here."

Angelina whistled. "That was two weeks ago, Joe."

The pathologist shrugged. "I haven't been outside. And I don't turn on the communicator any more. I don't *think* I was drunk the whole two weeks."

"Maybe I'd better make some coffee," Angelina offered.

"Coffee machine's broken." Dr. Aliotto couldn't take his eyes off the alien. "But you're speaking English—how can that be?"

"Learned it after I got here."

"Took him a whole week, the dummy," Angelina remarked.

Dr. Aliotto was clearly having trouble adjusting to the fact that a recognizable extraterrestrial life-form was sitting before him in his own quarters, chatting casually over drinks. "But where did you come from? What are you doing here?"

Zalmox grinned. "I come from a planet called Nisa in a star system you never heard of. I'm here to plant fruit trees. I'm not a spy for a war-mongering space race, nor do I carry any infectious diseases. I'm housebroken, reasonably well-spoken, and good company once you get to know me. And yes, thank you, I will have another."

Reminded, Dr. Aliotto took a swallow from his own glass. "You came alone?"

"All alone. Angelina?"

The black woman held out her glass.

"To plant fruit trees? You traveled from one planet to another planet *to plant fruit trees*?"

"Ah, but this is a very special fruit. Wait till you taste it. Speaking of tasting, this bottle seems to be empty. What do you call it? A dead sailor?"

"Soldier," corrected Angelina. "Got any more, Joe?" Dr.
Aliotto shook his head. "Well, no problem. We can go to the
Omph."

"What's an Omph?" asked Zalmox.

"We shall show you. Joe, go make yourself beautiful.
We're stepping out."

"I'll just get rid of this beard and—. Uh."

"What's the matter?"

"Depilatory machine's broken."

Jennie's easy stride took her up the foothills to the point
where a walk turned into a climb. *I wonder if anyone's ever
scaled this mountain*, she thought. Off to her right was one of
the two dozen consoles that had been sunk into mountain
rock—for the benefit of half-hearted nature lovers who
didn't really want to get out of touch with civilization.

She detoured to the console and activated the panel.
"Dan, has anyone ever climbed this mountain?"

"No, love. And don't you try it either."

"Why not?"

"Because you know absolutely nothing about mountain-
climbing."

"No, I mean why has no one ever climbed it?"

"No interest in it, I suppose. Pythians climb metaphoric
mountains and leave the physical derring-do to earthlings.
What are you doing out there, anyway?"

"Looking for God." She switched off.

She had gone only a few steps when Dan switched himself
back on. "Jennifer Geiss, that was positively *rude*! Come
back here and apologize!"

Jennie went back. "I am sorry, Dan. I've got the
mulligrubs today."

"Why aren't you down with the rest of them gawping at
the alien?"

"Are they gawping?"

In answer Dan activated the console screen and Jennie
found herself looking at the interior of the Omph. The place
was packed, but it wasn't hard to pick the alien out of the
crowd: his head and shoulders towered above everyone

around him. And it looked as if everyone were around him—clearly the center of interest, the alien was talking and smiling, completely at ease.

"Charming boy, Zalmox," said Dan. "We've had several nice little chats."

The stranger was leaving the Omph now, followed by several people—Angelina Baker, a couple of the Briles clone, Maya Indhara, and . . . who was that?

"Oh," said Jennie aloud, "I didn't know Dr. Aliotto was growing a beard."

Zalmox moved slowly, gracefully, surely not unaware of the overt glances of admiration directed his way.

"Have you talked to him yet?" asked Dan.

"No." Jennie said good-bye and headed up the mountain. She scrambled over some loose shale and—yes, there it was. A small secluded spot on the mountainside she had first discovered twenty years ago. It was warm, quiet, and private. A child's hidey-hole.

Jennie lay on her back and looked up at the patch of sky that was framed by the rocks around her hiding place. Her mouth opened in surprise at what she saw.

She saw a cloud.

In all the time she'd been with Barry, Jennie had never been able to talk him into fabricating a cloud. Why? he had asked. Their ecosystem didn't depend upon clouds for rain, so why spend all that time and work making what would be nothing more than a pretty decoration?

And yet there one was. Jennie watched it until it floated out of sight. She closed her eyes. *I wonder what made him change his mind.* Soon she was asleep.

She had been sleeping for almost an hour when a soft caress on her cheek redirected her dreams. From the empty museum she'd been wandering in, she suddenly found herself delivering a speech before the U.N. General Assembly. A second caress on the cheek and she opened her eyes.

The alien smiled down at her.

"I've been looking for you," he said.

Jennie sat up, slightly flustered. "How did you find me?"

"Through ingenuity, through perseverance, and by asking

Dan," he laughed and sat beside her. "I wanted to thank you for holding your hand out to me that first day. I wasn't sure anyone would."

Jennie smiled. "Oh, someone would have. I just happened to be there."

"Dr. Boyd happened to be there, too, but she wasn't what I'd call enthusiastic about seeing me."

"It's Thalia's job to exercise restraint."

"And what is your job?"

There was a short silence. "I don't have a job," Jennie finally answered.

The stranger stared at her in surprise, and then gave a resounding whoop of laughter. "Marvelous! I was beginning to think there wasn't a single person on this work-oriented planet who wasn't dedicated to the Great Plan."

Jennie was confused. "What Great Plan?"

"I don't know. But they all seem to think they're going somewhere."

Jennie laughed. "Oh, come on! You have work to do yourself. You're an agronomist, aren't you?"

He shrugged. "I put things in the ground, they grow. Anyone can do it. But why aren't you a part of all that extraordinary medical activity going on down there?"

Jennie explained why she missed the last ship, and told him about her two books and her tutoring chores.

"You're a writer and a teacher and you say you have no job?"

"I'm a poor writer and a worse teacher. It's all make-work anyway. What can you do, when your imagination is derivative?" A familiar bitter taste returned to her mouth. "No, I take it back. I do have a job. My function is to be the old-fashioned cliché every community needs to be complete. I am the outsider, suffering loudly and dramatically from feelings of estrangement and alienation from my society. I am the one who doesn't belong."

The stranger smiled at her gently. "I'd have thought that would be *my* function," he said.

"You're welcome to it." Time to change the subject. "Tell me, is Zalmox your complete name? We need at least two names here."

"No, I have many names. But since I seem to be the only Zalmox on Pythia, one will do. Unless there's a Zalmox Jones lurking around somewhere that I don't know about."

"No, you're quite safe." Jennie was aware of a delicate aroma coming from the body of the stranger next to her. It was not unpleasant.

"Look." Zalmox pointed to the sky. The cloud was floating by again. "A man named Barry Gomez made that. I mentioned I was surprised that Pythia had no clouds, and he offered to produce one. And that's what he did. He made *one* cloud."

Jennie laughed and stretched out on the ground. "Consider yourself fortunate. I couldn't get him to make even one."

Zalmox bent over her. "You and Barry are . . ."

"We were. Now we aren't." That aroma again. She reached up and fingered the gold curls on his head.

Suddenly they were making love. Jennie's hands slid over the stranger's smooth skin as she buried herself in his unique scent. Zalmox was an alien to whom she had spoken for the first time only ten minutes earlier, but she didn't stop to question the wisdom of giving herself to an intimacy she had not known with her other lovers. Never had there been the sense of *union* that Zalmox offered. She was frightened by the intensity of her own pleasure.

When two hours of love-making left her weak and exhausted, Zalmox took her in his arms and carried her down from the mountain.

It required no special insight for Pythia to understand what had happened. The new book was forgotten: Jennie spent most of her time with Zalmox, and he, in turn, made no attempt to hide his affection for her. Jennie found herself envied by—oddly enough—both men and women. Claude had looked at her strangely and then made himself invisible. But these things passed over her head; she was half-mad in her delight with Zalmox.

● ● ●

Thalia Boyd was not delighted.

"Jennie, have you stopped to think what you're doing? We know nothing about Zalmox, and don't tell me you know all you need to know about him."

"I wasn't going to. But it's my affair, isn't it?"

"Not quite. If you want to run around like a calf-eyed schoolgirl after a handsome man, that's your business. But we don't even know whether Zalmox *is* a man or not. And stop looking so smug; you know what I mean."

Jennie laughed. "I don't define a man in terms of his love-making ability. But I do think you're making an unnecessary fuss."

"We know nothing of his bodily make-up. What if you become pregnant? A pregnancy might be dangerous."

"I take my shots."

"Which neutralize *human* semen. They may be totally ineffective against Zalmox. Jennie, you haven't lived all your life on Pythia for nothing, I hope. Surely you can see the danger."

Jennie smiled. "I can see that you're worried, and I'm sorry, Thalia. I wish I could do something about that. But don't expect me to give up Zalmox. I won't. Ever."

Thalia rubbed her forehead in defeat. "Jennie, I don't even understand why you find him so attractive."

Jennie was surprised. "Zalmox? You don't understand why I find Zalmox attractive?" She thought *everybody* saw that.

"He's so...effeminate."

"*Effeminate!*"

"Yes, effeminate! With his sweet-smelling oiled skin and his pretty little yellow curls and his girlish way of walking. I wouldn't have thought that was your style."

Jennie was dumbfounded. "Are we talking about the same Zalmox? The one who arrived in a space ship about three weeks ago? That *epitome* of manhood?"

The two women stared at each other in disbelief.

Thalia gave Zalmox a section of land next to the animal compound where he could plant his fruit trees. The alien used a chemical auger to prepare the ground for the forced-growth process he used, but he insisted the trees be planted by hand.

Jennie sat on her heels as she watched her lover demonstrate the proper method of planting.

"It's not difficult," Zalmox was saying. "The roots require careful handling, that's all. See, like this." He picked up a miniature tree. "Insert your fingers among the roots—very, very carefully because the roots are fragile. Then spread the roots slowly, as far as you can. See?" He held out the tree so Jennie could inspect the spread roots; the tiny tendrils seemed to curl about Zalmox's fingers. "Now lower the tree into the ground, still spreading the roots. Use your other hand to brush in the soil. Don't pack it. When the tree can stand alone, work your fingers loose from the roots and remove your hand. Then pile in the rest of the soil—loosely, so it mounds up on top. The mound will sink into the hole gradually, feeding the tree without putting unnecessary pressure on the roots."

"How delicate it is!" exclaimed Jennie.

"As a matter of fact, it's quite hardy once the roots catch hold. It's only this first part that's tricky. Here, you try it."

Jennie tried it, breaking a tiny root on her first attempt. But soon she got the hang of it; and by the time she'd planted her third tree, there was a *rightness* to the feel of the roots twisting around her fingers that was oddly satisfying.

As she scooped the soil into a mound, a shadow fell over her hands. She looked up to see one very curious chimpanzee watching her. "Hello, Jacob. Have you come to help us?"

"We both have," said a voice from behind her. She looked back to see Dr. Tirsos smiling down at her. "Felt like playing hooky today," he confessed. "Show me how you do that."

Once again Zalmox described how to plant the fruit trees, but this time Jennie demonstrated. The little tree stood upright after only a few minutes.

Then the two newcomers tried it. Dr. Tirsos was slightly awkward, as was to be expected, but Jacob got his right on the first try. The scientist growled as the chimp grinned and flexed his agile human fingers.

Zalmox had prepared the land for planting not in the straight rows of conventional orchards, but in a zig-zag pattern. They would plant three trees, make a ninety-degree turn, plant three more, make another turn back in the original direction. Woman, chimpanzee, alien, elderly man—they worked in a line, moving in unison with a rhythm that soon filled Jennie with music. Softly, to herself at first, she began to sing.

When her song was ended, Jennie looked up to see they had attracted the attention of some passers-by. Jacob was showing three of the Briles clone how to spread the tree's roots. The twins were pestering Zalmox for "farmer lessons."

And Dr. Indhara was staring incredulously at Dr. Tirsos. "How can you do all that bending and stooping?" he asked. "With your back?"

Dr. Tirsos looked startled. He reached a hand around and touched the lower region of his spine. "Why," he said, "I'd forgotten all about it. It doesn't hurt at all. In fact, I haven't felt this good in a long time." He smiled in pleasure and picked up one of the trees. "Would you like to try planting one?"

"You're mad." Dr. Indhara smiled back.

"Do I look mad?"

"No, you look insufferably pleased with yourself. Here, give me that thing. If you can do it, so can I."

Jennie worked her zig-zag row for a while and then stopped for a breather. She looked around and was amazed at the number of people who had stopped to help. Little more than an hour had passed since Zalmox had first shown her the proper planting procedure, but now there were—oh, at least twenty people planting fruit trees. Jennie smiled to herself. None of these people were what you'd call back-to-the-soil types. The break in routine must have been highly welcome to attract so large a group.

"Who's minding the store?" Jennie asked Bert.

"Nobody," the pharmacist puffed.

So nobody was in the dispensary. So O.K.

Jennie bent back to her work, the now-familiar roots caressing her hand almost sensually. Voices called softly back and forth to each other; someone else began to sing. Jennie felt good. A sense of community existed; normal and experimental human, scientist and technician shared the strange and simple pleasure of planting fruit together.

Jacob placed the last tree in the ground just as the artificial daylight began to fade. Sweaty, dirty Pythians grinned at each other in satisfaction.

"Where are those boys?" said Zalmox. "I sent them for—ah, here they are."

Matt was pushing a wheeled platform on which rested a huge old-fashioned wooden keg. Eddie was straining under the burden of a large box that clinked as he walked.

"Beer for everybody," Zalmox called out. "Unless I'm the only one who's thirsty."

Several voices assured him he was not. Matt opened the tap and filled the steins which Eddie passed around. The beer was cold and good, and welcome. Dr. Tirsos and Dr. Indhara were the first to ask for refills. The two elderly scientists were seated on the ground, relaxed and enjoying themselves.

"Where's Bert?" asked Zalmox.

"He went into the animal compound to find a place to wash his hands," said Jennie. "He can't stand being grubby."

"Hey! Did I miss something?" It was Sam Flaherty.

"Yeah, Aquaman, you missed something." That was Eddie.

"But have a beer anyway," smiled Zalmox. "You understand, of course, that come harvest time you will be expected to pay for your brew with the sweat of your brow."

"Of course! Just gimme a beer. I will labor later."

Jacob held out his slate. *He wouldn't know how*, it said.

"When do you expect harvest, Zalmox?" asked Dr. Indhara.

"In six weeks."

"Six weeks! That's incredible. We can force-grow a tree in a year—but six weeks! What chemicals are you using? May I have a sample to test?"

"Certainly. As much as you want."

"Well, look at that, will you?" Jennie exclaimed. "Bert has found a friend."

The pharmacist was hurrying through an enclosure of the animal compound, trying to shoo away a donkey that trotted along behind him.

The group laughed. At the enclosure gate Bert tried to slip

through, but the donkey butted at him gently with its head. Bert gave up and let the animal through. "He followed me home, Ma. Can I keep him?"

Eddie handed Bert three beers.

"Why three?"

"You're behind."

"Oh. Well, we can't have that, can we?" He chugalugged all three beers, a feat which drew applause but which left Bert slightly pop-eyed.

Matt held a full stein under the donkey's nose. A long tongue started slapping at the beer.

Bert threw his arm around the donkey's neck. "Attaboy," he said as he reached for his fourth beer.

"Easy, Bert," Dr. Tirsos cautioned. "You've been sweating a lot, and too much beer too fast—"

"Makes you healthy, wealthy, and wise," Bert finished as he drained the stein.

"Why didn't I know you were all playing farmer today?" Sam complained.

Jacob handed him his slate. *Because you're stupid.*

Sam roared in mock fury and lunged at the chimp, who scampered away and sat in the lap of one of the Briles girls.

"What's the matter?" Jennie asked Eddie.

The twin was scowling at his stein. "Why don't I like this stuff?"

Matt silently picked up Jacob's slate and handed it to his brother.

"I like orchards," said Zalmox, gazing back over the newly planted land.

"Yeah," said Bert. "Without orchards, we wouldn't have beer."

"Beer comes from orchards?" laughed Zalmox.

"As far as I'm concerned, *this* beer comes from *this* orchard, and I'd like some more, please."

"How come your speech is clear when your face is so slurred?" asked Eddie as he refilled Bert's stein.

"I dunno. Ask Dr. Tirsos."

Dr. Tirsos just shrugged.

"I wish my wife were here," said Dr. Indhara.

"I wish *I* were here," said Bert.

Matt belched. "'Scuse me."

"I gotta pee," said Sam.

"Not on my trees," said Zalmox.

Jennie stood up. "Do you really think you ought to try that, Bert?"

The pharmacist had one leg over the donkey's back and was trying to hoist himself up. "I could use a little help," he grunted.

The twins stationed themselves on either side of the donkey. Matt put his shoulder to Bert's backside and gave him a boost and the pharmacist almost toppled over on the other side, but Eddie was there to steady him.

"Giddap," said Bert.

The donkey didn't move.

Bert started wobbling, but Eddie and Matt quickly had him steady again. The donkey was wearing a bridle that had no reins attached to it; Bert looked around for something to do with his hands and ended up placing them on the twins' heads.

"In the name of the father and the son and the holy smoke," he intoned, "I anoint you Bert-supporters."

"Better get him home," Dr. Tirsos said.

Jacob took hold of the donkey's bridle and tugged at it. The donkey began to move.

The others fell in behind. It would take more than two boys and a chimpanzee to get Bert tucked away.

"Music!" commanded Bert from the head of the procession.

Jennie activated the nearest wall panel. "Are you watching this, Dan?"

"With *utter* fascination."

"Well, the man wants music."

"And music he shall have."

For some reason Dan chose a German oom-pah band, and the brassy music blared from the speakers. Bert made the mistake of trying to conduct the band from donkey-back and almost took a spill. But steadying hands kept him upright.

As the procession neared Bert's quarters, Dan switched to a lullaby.

"Oh, wow," Jennie said. "How cornball can you get?"

"Wait," said Zalmox. "It might work."

By the time Jacob stopped the donkey in front of Bert's quarters, the pharmacist was sound asleep, propped up by the twins, smiling as he slept.

"Well, you're home early," Maya Indhara said.

"I've been home for an hour," her husband answered.

"Why? Is something wrong?"

"No, I just decided to quit early."

Surprised, Maya sat down beside him. "For the last fifteen years I've been trying to get you to work shorter hours. Are you feeling all right?"

Dr. Indhara laughed. "I'm feeling fine. In fact, I feel so good that from now on my work day is going to be considerably shorter. There's really no need for me to hover over everything that's done in that laboratory. I'm going to turn most of the checking-up over to someone else."

His wife was momentarily speechless with astonishment. "Are you serious?"

"Never more serious in my life."

Maya Indhara uttered a tiny cry of pleasure and leaned over to kiss her husband's nose—a gesture she hadn't made in ten years.

"And now," Dr. Indhara said, "what about you? Is it really necessary for you to spend so much time in the O.R.?"

"Sorry I've been such a sorehead," said Dr. Aliotto.

"Forget it." Angelina Baker smiled.

"No, I mean it. I've been snarling at everybody—even you. And I really am sorry. Forgive me."

"Nothing to forgive."

"I get too excited about things. That business with Thalia Boyd—it can be worked out somehow."

"Sure it can."

"I don't know why I carried on that way. It's not that important."

Angelina breathed a sigh of relief. "I was getting worried about you, Joe; I wasn't sure you'd rejoin the human race."

"I wasn't so sure I wanted to—for a while, at any rate. Angelina, I owe you."

"Me? Why?"

"Because you brought Zalmox to me and kept on beating on the door until I had to open it. If you hadn't made that effort, I'd have just gone on feeling sorry for myself and sinking lower and lower. You stopped all that, and I'm grateful. I want you to know that."

"I understand." They both were silent a moment. Then: "I kinda like your beard. Makes you look like a satyr."

"Really? Then I must practice my leer."

"You can use my mirror," said Angelina.

Adelbert watched Sam Flaherty carefully while explaining the problem the new pharmaceutical machines would cause him. Time was running out; soon Bert would have to decide whether to go or stay. He wondered if he could make this casual, self-centered young experimental understand what it meant to be automated out of a job.

"You know what I think?" said Sam. "I think you worry too much. You say you'll be forty-four when your next gig is up. Then stay and enjoy an easy nine years. Who knows what you'll want to do in nine years?"

"But I have to plan ahead."

"Why? Say you go back to Earth and learn a new profession. What guarantee do you have that *that* line of work won't be automated by the time you've mastered it? These things aren't in your control. Don't try to buck it; just ride with it."

"That sounds like what used to be called 'copping out.'"

"No, I don't think it is." Sam thought for a moment. "Look, Bert, I'm in about the same situation. I'm a lame duck too."

"*You* are?"

"Sure. Only I don't have a choice about where I live. My webbing has been the most successful of all such experiments attempted here. As a result, I can outswim everybody on Pythia. Swell. Would Earth let me into the Olympics? No, my value is here, where stress and strain on the webbing can be tested until everybody's satisfied with it. Meanwhile, there are half a dozen children running around who've been given the lungs that work underwater. If those lungs hold up over the years, the next step is to combine the two experiments. *Then* they'll have a practical combination—underwater workers will no longer have to fool with fins and air tanks and all the rest of it. But that won't be me, Bert. That'll be somebody else."

The pharmacist looked at the young man with concern. He'd never even thought about what might lie in Sam Flaherty's future.

"So you see," Sam continued, "I'm a kind of dry run. My usefulness is even more short-lived than yours. But this is where I belong, and this is where I'm going to stay. Where would you rather live, Bert—here or on Earth?"

"Here, I think. I have no family. Going back to Earth would mean going back to a changed world to live among strangers. Pythia isn't ideal, but at least I know people here."

"Then stay. The future has a way of taking care of itself. Don't think I'm being glib—I don't mean to be. From what I understand about the way things are on Earth, this search for job satisfaction is practically a hereditary *malaise* that almost always seems to end in failure. Am I wrong?"

Bert hesitated a moment, and then said, "No, you're not wrong."

"Then why go through all that grief? Who needs it?"

"You may be right. But it's not exactly easy to throw over a career like that."

"I suppose not." Then Sam grinned awkwardly. "But I hope you stay. We're kind of used to seeing you around."

The admission embarrassed Sam, but Bert was grateful to him for making it.

It was the word he needed.

Thalia Boyd punched the same series of buttons for the third time with no result. Impatiently, she hit the large red button in the center of the control panel.

"You rang?" said Dan.

"Something's wrong with the communicator. I've been

trying to get Dr. Tirsos and nothing happens."

"Oh? I'll look into it." Two minutes later he said, "A simple parts breakdown; I've initiated repair. Must have overlooked it; sorry. I called Dr. Tirsos on another channel and—ta-*taa!*—here he is."

Dr. Tirsos's face appeared on the viewscreen.

"I thought you'd like to know I've decided not to approve the pseudoluciferin experiments," Thalia said. "The last tests the team conducted offer nothing new in the way of proof one way or the other. We'll just go with Occam's Razor and look for a theory with fewer assumptions in it."

Dr. Tirsos nodded. "Very well. One of the team members is here now; I'll tell him."

"Thanks. I hate to disappoint them, but—"

"I wouldn't worry about it, if I were you. They seem to have lost interest."

"*Lost interest?*"

"Well, perhaps that's putting it too strongly. But I don't think they'll be as disappointed as they would have been earlier. Enthusiasm does wane, sometimes."

Puzzled, Thalia thanked him and switched off.

A thought nudged Jennie: *What about Claude?* For almost six weeks she had given no thought to her former lover, but now she was surprised to find that she missed him. She could be quiet and comfortable with Claude in a way Zalmox's priapine sexuality made impossible. Zalmox was shock therapy; Claude was a tranquillizer. One lover at a time was enough for Jennie—but still, she missed Claude.

She would go see him. She didn't think she wanted to apologize; she just wanted to see him. He might refuse to talk to her, but somehow Jennie didn't think he would.

Claude's quarters were located on the far side of the colony from her own. She opened his door and stepped into the living area. Nothing had changed from the last time she'd been there, and she would have been surprised if it had. Claude was the only person she knew who could live in the same place for over eight years without leaving the stamp of his own personality on his surroundings.

Jennie stopped cold: a low laugh from the bedroom had just reached her ear. Turn around *right now* and get out of here, she told herself.

She didn't listen to herself. Like one being hauled in on an invisible rope, Jennie moved toward the bedroom. If that's Cynthia Howell he's got in there, she thought, I do believe I'll scream.

It wasn't Cynthia Howell. It was Zalmox.

Fascinated, Jennie stood in the doorway watching the two men. They were nude, their legs wrapped around each other. Claude held Zalmox cradled in his arms and was kissing him gently as if he were a woman. Jennie's alien-lover lay relaxed, graceful, receptive. Suddenly Thalia Boyd's picture of Zalmox made sense: he was clearly the "feminine" partner in this relationship.

A part of her mind told Jennie she should feel shocked, betrayed. But the greater part of her mind ate in the scene hungrily. The sight of the male love-making affected her strangely: she stepped forward into the room.

Zalmox and Claude looked up and said "Jennie!" at exactly the same time—smiling, not the least bit flustered. *They were glad to see her.*

"You're just what we need," said Zalmox.

"Your timing couldn't be better," said Claude.

The rope drew her toward them. What am I doing? she asked herself. Something I want to do, she answered.

Four arms reached for her.

The next night, Claude moved in with Jennie.

"Might as well forget about it," Dan yawned. "Nobody's going to show."

Dr. Tirsos didn't answer. This was the first time in his long career that *all* his assistants had failed to appear for work.

"Why don't you take the day off too? You can't handle a rewire by yourself," Dan said in his most persuasive tones.

Even cyborgs enjoyed an occasional unscheduled vacation.

"The new wiring is needed for an experiment tomorrow," said Dr. Tirsos.

"So experiment the day after tomorrow. If anyone still wants to."

"Where is everybody?"

"Here and there. Relaxing. Summer doldrums, you know."

"It isn't summer."

"Picky, picky. It's close enough. Take off your shoes and run barefoot through the grass. Do you good."

Dr. Tirsos frowned and left. Clearly Dan was going to be no help.

Outside Dr. Tirsos headed toward the animal compound. There seemed to be people everywhere—more than he could remember ever seeing together at once out of doors. And they were all doing what Dan had said they were doing: relaxing. No pressures, no tensions, no hurry-hurry. And no work getting done.

He passed the animal compound and went into the field where he had helped plant Zalmox's trees. Every day he made the trip to inspect the trees that would allegedly produce a new healing agent. And every day he marveled at the rapidity with which they were shooting up; Pythia had no forced-growth process to match this one.

And today—yes! There they were! Little globules forming on the branches. Green with (*already*?) a slight pink tinge forming.

It wouldn't be long now.

"You want to write a play about *me*?" asked Zalmox.

"You said it, big man." Eddie grinned happily. "You're the biggest thing that's happened in our innocent young lives."

"How innocent?" asked Zalmox.

"Enough. Would you prefer to speak immortal blank verse or peerless prose?"

"I'll take a little of each."

"A proper and fitting answer. We will make you a Bringer of Light—"

Zalmox shuddered.

"—or would you rather be the Sping of Kace? Whoops! I mean King of Space."

"What's that called—what you just did? Is that a spoonerism?"

"Yes. Some spoonerisms are permissible, such as speaking of Wordsworth's dimple siction instead of his simple diction. But special caution must be exercised when mentioning 'Pippa Passes', Puck and the fairies, or 'Folly's Mart.'"

Zalmox turned to Matt. "Why do you let your brother do all the talking?"

"I'm a ventriloquist," said Matt.

Cynthia Howell entered her quarters and noticed the message light flashing on the control board. She pressed the receive button and Dan's voice boomed out at her.

"Cynthia, Barry wants you to know he had to go to the weather tower to check a faulty generator I told him about. He says he doesn't know how long he'll be and you're not to worry if he's late getting back. Also, he loves you very much, and how I hate delivering mushy messages like this!"

"Thank you, Dan," Cynthia smiled.

She was pleased. Two months ago it would never have occurred to Barry to leave a message for her. He used to get annoyed whenever she worried about him. Now he was daily becoming more loving and considerate. A much *nicer* man than he used to be.

And that was odd, for Cynthia was almost certain Barry knew she'd slept with Zalmox. But Barry seemed to bear no animosity toward either of them—in fact, he and the alien had become close friends lately. The friendship had had a gentling influence on Barry that made him more dear to her than ever.

One way or another, Zalmox's arrival on Pythia had been good for both of them.

• • •

Zalmox plucked a reddish-purple globe from a tree and split it open. "Yes," he said. "They're ready."

A murmur of anticipation ran through the group that had gathered to harvest the fruit. They moved out among the trees and began picking.

"Hey!" Eddie yelled to Sam Flaherty. "Don't just *throw* them in the bin; they'll bruise."

"No, they won't," called Zalmox. "Just don't squeeze them and they'll be all right."

Sam stuck his tongue out at the twin.

Thalia Boyd stood watching. "I hope you told them not to sample the fruit until we've had a chance to analyze it."

"They know," said Zalmox. "Where's Dr. Tirsos?"

"Working."

The trees were so heavily laden that it took a worker over an hour to strip just one tree. The first bin filled was hustled off to Dr. Indhara's laboratory for analysis. The rest would be stored to await the result of the lab tests.

It was clearly going to be an all-day job, even with the large turn-out the harvest had attracted. Thalia ran her eye over the group gathering the fruit and estimated that fully half of them were supposed to be working elsewhere. She started back to her office, and then stopped.

"You know not to taste the fruit, don't you, Jacob?" she said.

The chimp nodded and went on shaking a branch of his tree. One of the globes of fruit that fell to the ground rolled to her feet. Thalia picked it up and examined it.

Coarse outer skin—couldn't be bitten through. She pierced the skin with her fingernail and peeled back the outer layer to reveal the soft purplish pulp underneath. A sweet-sour aroma—rather interesting. She took the fruit with her.

When Thalia returned late in the day she found most of the pickers looking a bit sheepish. Jacob had brought three other chimpanzees with him, and the chimps had easily out-picked the humans. But the crop had been harvested: bins filled with fruit stood among the zig-zag lines of trees.

"All finished," Zalmox greeted Thalia. "The trees are stripped and in good condition for the second growth."

"Second growth?"

"Yes. In about two weeks there'll be another crop."

"Zalmox, I have Dr. Indhara's report. It seems there are two elements in your fruit he can't identify."

Jennie Geiss came up to join them.

"Probably elements not indigenous to Pythia or Earth," Zalmox said. "I can identify them for him."

"We'll still have to test them out."

"They're not harmful. Nothing in the fruit is."

"But we still have only your word for that, don't we?" said Thalia.

Jennie frowned.

"So test away," Zalmox shrugged. "How will you do it?"

"First on mice, probably. Ultimately on Dan."

"And how long will that take?"

"Oh, we'll hurry, Zalmox. How fast does your fruit rot?"

Jennie took a purple globe from one of the bins.

"Not fast, Dr. Boyd. Not fast at all. It can last a long time, if conditions are right."

"And are conditions right?"

"I would say they were almost perfect."

Thalia took a deep breath. "You may be right. But nobody eats that fruit until it's tested on Dan."

"You can skip Dan," said Jennie, wiping a purple stain from her mouth. "Start with me."

Thalia felt her stomach sink. "Oh, Jennie," she said accusingly.

"Then what happened?" asked Dr. Tirsos.

"For half an hour, nothing. Then," said Thalia simply, "she went mad."

Dr. Tirsos frowned at the imprecision of the term. "What did she do?"

"Well, she laughed. She laughed and laughed. And then she started breaking things—we had her in Dr. Indhara's lab, and she started smashing equipment. Every time she broke something, she laughed harder. A simple destructive binge we could have coped with, but that laughter was something else. It threw us all for a loop. Dr. Tirsos, I was afraid of her. Actually afraid. Of Jennie. Can you imagine such a thing?"

He shook his head.

"Then she started throwing things. When a microscope came sailing in my direction, I ducked under a lab table. When I came back out, she'd gone into the next room. Evidently Dr. Indhara tried to stop her, and do you know what she did? She grabbed his balls."

Dr. Tirsos's eyebrows shot up. "What did Indhara do?"

"According to Cynthia Howell, he ran like a scared rabbit."

Dr. Tirsos permitted a small smile.

"Well, eventually we were able to restrain her," Thalia went on. "I've got her in confinement now, still laughing like a maniac. Some 'cure' for schizophrenia!"

"What does Zalmox have to say?"

"That arrogant pretty-boy had the nerve to tell me I handled it wrong. 'Her fit will pass,' he said—as if that were all that mattered! Why, she could have injured herself the way she was going on—not to mention the danger she posed to other people. Zalmox said we should have just let her run loose."

Dr. Tirsos's forehead creased into a frown. "I'm not sure I always understand that young man."

Thalia snorted. "He's an obstructionist. Claude Billings was able to get a sample of Jennie's blood before we locked her up. Dr. Indhara's team is working on developing an antidote right now, but they're up against those two unknown elements, remember. And Zalmox refuses to help! He keeps saying there's no need for an antidote. No need! Ye gods."

"I'll clear one of Dan's life-support systems so we can test as soon as Indhara's ready."

"Good. And then," said Thalia, "then we must decide what to do about Zalmox."

The bins of fruit were safely locked up—not that there was much likelihood of further sampling by the Pythians.

Everyone was frightened by what had happened to Jennie.

A day passed and Dr. Indhara still had no antidote. Zalmox kept insisting no antidote was needed, that Jennie was all right. Dan told Thalia to listen to Zalmox. Thalia told Dan to butt out.

"So what happens now?" Angelina asked, inviting herself into Thalia's office.

"So we pray a lot," said Thalia. "If Dr. Indhara can't come up with an antidote, Zalmox is the only one with the answer."

"And how do you plan on getting an answer out of him?"

Thalia paused a moment. "Know anything about torture?"

The black woman smiled in sympathy. "You know, Thalia, Zalmox does say Jennie's seizure will pass. I don't like watching something like this happening. I especially don't like the thought of two unidentified elements racing around in that girl's bloodstream. But could he possibly be right?"

"Not only could be, but is," said a voice behind them.

The two women swiveled to see a relaxed, happy Jennie Geiss standing in the doorway.

Thalia moved toward her quickly. "How do you feel? Have you regained control?" *How did you get out.*

"I never felt better," laughed Jennie. "I mean that literally, Thalia. *I never felt better.*"

The two physicians looked at each other. "Do you keep anything here?" asked Angelina.

"Behind that panel," Thalia pointed.

"What are you talking about?" asked Jennie.

Angelina removed a few pieces of medical equipment from behind the panel Thalia had indicated and began taking Jennie's blood pressure. Thalia made several calls on the communicator.

"She seems to be in good shape," said Angelina after a brief examination.

"Jennie," said Thalia, "I've just made arrangements for you to be given a complete checkup. We're going to give you every test we know and maybe even invent a few new ones. You look great, but you understand we have to be sure."

"Of course," smiled Jennie. "I want you to be sure." (Not,

Thalia noticed, "I want to be sure myself.") "I vaguely remember breaking things. I'm terribly sorry about that, and of course I'll make good the damage."

Thalia waved this aside impatiently. "That's not important, Jennie. What's important is your physical condition."

"My physical condition couldn't be better," she smiled confidently. "You'll see. And by the way, if you ever plan on placing someone in confinement again, you'd better change the locks. The one in my door must have been put together by the original Liverpudlian Jerry brothers. I merely touched it and it fell apart."

"That's how you got out?"

"That's how I got out."

The three women sat grinning at one another.

"Honey," Angelina said to Jennie, "I can't tell you how good you're looking."

Jennie's self-diagnosis proved to be accurate.

Not only was she in excellent physical condition, but also no traces of the two unknown elements could be found in her blood. Whatever had triggered the hysteria had passed out of her system.

And left a changed Jennie Geiss in its wake. Jennie was poised and calm now—even serene. Thalia watched Jennie carefully and could see no sign whatever of the depression that habitually lurked so near Jennie's rather transparent surface. The little-girl-who-was-left-behind aura had disappeared.

The rest of Pythia was watching Jennie too. Her emergence as a quiet, self-confident woman scored points for Zalmox: he obviously knew what he was talking about. After Jennie's recovery, Zalmox had proved willing to identify the two elements in the fruit that were not known to the Pythians. Dr. Indhara was working to find a repressor for the first and violent stage of the assimilative process that would not inhibit the calming stage: bypass war and go directly to peace. Zalmox doubted that such a selective repressor existed.

It was almost time for the second-growth harvest; the

globules had already begun to form. This time, Thalia knew, the Pythians wouldn't be so agreeable about not sampling the wares. She wasn't at all sure she could enforce her *caveat* against alien fruit.

Something else bothered her. She wasn't convinced that Jennie had told her the whole truth about the way she escaped the confinement room. Those rooms weren't jerry-built, and that story about the lock's falling apart was more than a trifle far-fetched. Thalia wondered if Zalmox had engineered her release.

Several Pythians had indicated they would be willing to volunteer as experimental subjects if Thalia would unlock the fruit. At first Thalia had brushed off such suggestions casually. But as the days passed the requests increased in number to the point where she felt she was being pressured. It was a new kind of pressure, different from the normal high pressures of her job—and she didn't like it. Not at all.

Jennie lay on her back, trying to hold herself still as Claude tickled the soles of her feet with a blade of grass. When finally she couldn't stand it any longer, she laughed and pulled her feet away.

"You know what we should do?" Zalmox asked. "We should have a party."

Claude glanced around the mountainside, which every day attracted a few more Pythians. "Seems to me we're doing fine right now."

"No, I mean a *big* party. With everybody on Pythia invited."

"Including Thalia Boyd?"

"Especially Thalia Boyd."

"She won't come, Zalmox," said Jennie.

"Perhaps not. But wouldn't it be a gas? Everybody on the planet celebrating at the same time."

"Celebrating what?"

"Well, let's see." Zalmox thought a minute. "How about Vasco da Gama's birthday?"

Jennie laughed. "Where did you learn about Vasco da Gama?"

"From Eddie and Matt."

"Say, Zalmox," Barry Gomez said, leaning over a small boulder. "Dr. Boyd just came on one of the consoles and said she wants you to come to her office."

"All right, Barry," said Zalmox lazily. "Thanks."

"She said *right now* and she said it mean."

"I tremble in anticipation."

Barry grinned and disappeared behind the boulder.

"Hey, Zalmox!" Eddie called, laboring up a small incline.

"I know, I know. Barry just told me."

"Oh." Breathless, the twin plopped down at Jennie's feet.

"I wish," said Jennie, gazing up, "I wish Barry would make a playmate for his cloud. That one looks so lonely up there."

" 'I wandered lonely as a cloud—' " Eddie began to recite.

"Eddie," Claude interrupted, "you remember telling Zalmox about Vasco da Gama?"

"Yeah. Why?"

"Well, he thinks we ought to celebrate da Gama's birthday. A party. All Pythia to be invited. What do you think of that?"

"I think it's great!" Then the boy's grin gave way to a puzzled expression. "When *is* Vasco da Gama's birthday?"

"Who knows?" laughed Claude.

"I'll ask Dan," Eddie volunteered.

"Don't," said Jennie. "Let's pick our own day. I believe in movable birthdays."

"Fine with me," Eddie agreed. "I nominate today. Right now."

"It can't be today," said Zalmox as he got to his feet. "Right now it's time for me to play out my obligatory scene with Thalia Boyd."

ENTROPY ENTERPRISES

presents

AS THE UNIVERSE EXPANDS

(No. 2038)

Today's Episode: *The Obligatory Scene*

CHARACTERS:
DR. THALIA BOYD   DR. INDHARA
ZALMOX   CYNTHIA HOWELL
DR. TIRSOS   GIRL (MASHA)
TECHNICIAN   PICNICKERS

TEASER

FADE IN:

1   PYTHIA OVERVIEW (STOCK)   1

2   INT. — THALIA BOYD'S OFFICE   2

THALIA, DR. TIRSOS, and ZALMOX are seated around a small table. Zalmox is here to answer questions, Thalia to ask them, and Dr. Tirsos to back her up. Zalmox is the most relaxed of the three.

3   CLOSER ANGLE   3

                    THALIA

There are questions we simply must have answers to. You understand that your answers are being recorded?

                    ZALMOX

Yes.

                    THALIA

And I must warn you that I'm going to insist upon straight answers this time. Every time we've spoken before, you've been evasive and ambiguous.

                    ZALMOX

I'm sorry you think so. I have always tried to be truthful. Perhaps I can help a little right now by

stating that Dan's ideas are completely his own. I
suggested nothing to him.

DR. TIRSOS
Dan? What does Dan have to do with this?

ZALMOX
Haven't you noticed a change in him lately?

THALIA
(*A beat*)
Dr. Tirsos?

DR. TIRSOS
No, I haven't noticed a difference. What are you
talking about, Zalmox?

ZALMOX
I think he's beginning to feel discontent with
his ... circumstances.

DR. TIRSOS
That's hard to believe. Dan's psychological condition is under constant surveillance. I would have
been notified of any change.

THALIA
A diversionary tactic, Zalmox? We're here to ask
you questions, if you remember.

ZALMOX
Very well.

CUT TO:

4   VIEWING SCREEN — TECHNICIAN   4

TECHNICIAN
Dr. Boyd, is Dr. Tirsos with you?

5   WIDER ANGLE TO INCLUDE THALIA,   5
     DR. TIRSOS, ZALMOX

                    THALIA
Yes, he's here. What is it?

                  TECHNICIAN
Dr. Tirsos, I think you'd better come over here.
Dan... Dan is...

                  DR. TIRSOS
Dan is what? What's the matter?

                  TECHNICIAN
I... I'm not really sure. Dr. Tirsos, I wish you'd
examine him yourself.

                  DR. TIRSOS
Thalia —

                    THALIA
Of course. Go ahead.

6   ANGLE ON DR. TIRSOS, LEAVING   6

                  DR. TIRSOS
I'll get back to you as soon as I can.
                  (*Leaves*)

7   ANOTHER ANGLE — THALIA, ZALMOX   7

                    THALIA
And now, suppose you tell me what it is you've been
saying to Dan.

                              FADE OUT.

                  END TEASER

ACT ONE

FADE IN:

8   INT. THALIA'S OFFICE — THALIA, ZALMOX   8

> **ZALMOX**
> Please try to understand. I have said nothing to Dan that hasn't been said to him hundreds of times before. I've simply been listening.

> **THALIA**
> Then what's wrong with him?

> **ZALMOX**
> I'm not sure anything *is* wrong with him. He's merely beginning to look at things differently. To develop a new perspective.

> **THALIA**
> Oh, that's deep! Dan is undergoing a philosophical transmogrification that only you can see? Is that right?

> **ZALMOX**
> (*A beat*)
> Dr. Boyd, have you ever examined the reasons behind your hostility toward me?

> **THALIA**
> (*Bluntly*)
> Yes. And now I want some answers. Where are you from?

ZALMOX

Nisa. As you know, it's not on your charts.

THALIA

Nor anyone else's, I imagine. How did you break
our shield?

ZALMOX

Your protection isn't as strong as you think.

9   ANGLE ON THALIA   9

THALIA

Another evasive answer. Metaphorical, ominous-
sounding, but most of all, slippery.
                    (*Insisting*)
How did you break the shield!

ZALMOX'S VOICE

I didn't "break" it. Your shield is in the same
condition it has always been. I left no gap in your
protection, such as it is.

THALIA

Such as it is.

10   REVERSE ANGLE — ZALMOX   10

ZALMOX

Dr. Boyd, you and I both know your concern over
my unorthodox arrival is merely a cover for what's
really bothering you. You resent my presence here.
You oppose me at every turn. You've locked up my
fruit. You locked up Jennie Geiss—even when I
told you her seizure would pass. You labeled me
"villain" the moment you saw me and ever since you
have refused to consider any other possibility. You
are a scientist. Scientists investigate first, conclude

later. Do you think that's what you've done? Are you being true to your own standards?

11   WIDER ANGLE — THALIA, ZALMOX   11

THALIA
(*A beat*)
I think so. But I'll admit I may have overlooked something. I'm willing to listen. If you're willing to talk.

ZALMOX
Will you come with me?

THALIA
Where?

ZALMOX
For a short walk. Do you think you could look at Pythia with new eyes?
(*Thalia looks a question*)
All the great discoveries in the history of your species have been made by people looking at familiar things as if they'd never seen them before. Newton watching a falling apple. Galileo gazing at a swinging chandelier. Will you try to look at Pythia like that? As if it were completely new to you?

THALIA
With you as my guide, of course.
(*Zalmox smiles*)
All right, Zalmox. I'll come with you.

ZALMOX
Good.

DISSOLVE TO:

12   INT. LABORATORY   12

13 ANGLE ON DR. INDHARA   13
    AND CYNTHIA HOWELL, WORKING;
    THALIA AND ZALMOX SOME
    DISTANCE BEHIND THEM,
    WATCHING.

14 TWO SHOT — THALIA, ZALMOX   14

                    ZALMOX
Don't speak to them. Just watch.

                    THALIA
This is spying, Zalmox.

                    ZALMOX
"Spying" is one way of seeing with new eyes. Watch.

15 TWO SHOT — DR. INDHARA, CYNTHIA   15

    *Cynthia is holding a rack into which Dr. Indhara
    is placing test tubes.*

16 INSERT: INDHARA'S HANDS (TREMBLING), 16
    AND CYNTHIA'S HANDS, STEADY.

17 TWO SHOT — INDHARA, CYNTHIA   17

    *Cynthia puts away the test-tube rack as Indhara
    turns back to his lab table.*

                    DR. INDHARA
Cynthia, I need some more K-Alfaline.

                    CYNTHIA
I'll get it.

18 ANOTHER ANGLE   18

    *Cynthia moves some portable steps to a storage
    area. When she climbs the steps to reach up for the*

*K-Alfaline, Dr. Indhara walks over and looks up
the skirt of her lab uniform.*

19   CLOSE ANGLE ON THALIA,   19
     ZALMOX

                         THALIA
So an old man lusts after a young girl. This is the
"new" view of Pythia you wanted me to have?

                         ZALMOX
     Watch.

20   ANGLE ON DR. INDHARA   20

*He fumbles with his equipment, drops something
and breaks it.*

                     DR. INDHARA
Damn!

21   WIDER ANGLE TO INCLUDE   21
     CYNTHIA

                        CYNTHIA
     Dr. Indhara!

                     DR. INDHARA
It's ruined. The whole goddam thing is ruined. I'm
sorry, Cynthia. We'll have to start over.

                                  DISSOLVE TO:

22   TRANSITION SHOT — PARK, DAY   22

23   CAMERA TRACKS THALIA   23
     AND ZALMOX WALKING
     THROUGH PARK

THALIA

So what was that supposed to prove?

ZALMOX

That frustrated people make inefficient workers.

THALIA
(Amused)

Remarkable discovery! And I'll wager you have an equally remarkable solution.

ZALMOX

Not so remarkable. Simply do away with the causes of frustration. That's all.

THALIA
(Laughs)

Oh, is that all?

ZALMOX

It's not so difficult as you like to think. Dr. Indhara is suppressing his natural urges under an overlay of shame. He can't even look at Cynthia Howell without feeling guilty about his wife — whom he loves. All that frustration, anxiety — and it's so unnecessary. Cynthia is an open, loving girl who would be happy to accommodate Indhara. And it would have nothing to do with his wife. Think how many ruined experiments could be avoided.

THALIA
(Stops walking; faces Zalmox directly)

Accommodate him? Did you say "accommodate"? Is she to be used for Indhara's pleasure?

ZALMOX

Aren't we all sources of pleasure to one another now and then? And Cynthia has unplanned-for

physical needs too. Everyone does, of course.
Surely you have taken lovers since your husband's
death.

24   CLOSE ANGLE ON THALIA   24

THALIA

You are presumptuous. My private life is just that
— private. But I will tell you this: I have never
allowed myself to be used as a means of accommo-
dation. What you're suggesting is that Cynthia
Howell allow Dr. Indhara to use her body to
masturbate with. And that it's right for her to do so!

25   REVERSE ANGLE ON ZALMOX   25

ZALMOX

"Right" has nothing to do with it. I'm talking about
what is *necessary*.
          (*A short pause*)
Jennie Geiss told me about two of the early sex
researchers on your home planet. They offered the
advice that we should all approach sex the same
way we approach eating a meal. Eat when you are
hungry, not when the clock tells you it's time for a
meal. Now that sounds sensible, but it doesn't offer
any real help, does it? What if one partner is hungry
when the other isn't? Does the hungry partner then
go without the sustenance he or she needs?
          (*Moves closer to Thalia*)
If we don't eat, we die.

26   REVERSE ANGLE ON THALIA   26

THALIA

And what about the partner who isn't hungry?
Must that one force down unwanted food? What
about the right to say no? Or are you suggesting that
the hungry partner simply move on to a different
table?

(*Takes a step back*)

Zalmox, you asked me earlier about my hostility toward you. This is why. You advocate a life of wallowing self-indulgence. If we followed your lead, we'd spend all our time eating and drinking and screwing. And letting our minds stagnate. Sexual frustration isn't the only kind of frustration there is, you know. What about intellectual frustration?

27   ANGLE WIDENS TO INCLUDE ZALMOX   27

ZALMOX

What a premium you place on the intellect! Dr. Boyd, you must allow for what you so scornfully call "self-indulgence." You can't live under tight control all the time.

THALIA

Nor do I expect to. I understand the value of pressure valves. But what you advocate is not an occasional letting-off of steam, but a way of life. A constant catering to the senses, a destruction of form. You preach a doctrine of suicide.

ZALMOX
(*A beat*)

All I want is to see you happy.

THALIA

Then leave! Get in your ship and fly away and leave Pythia alone.

ZALMOX

I don't think that will make you happy.

THALIA

I doubt if you're capable of understanding this, but I *was* happy. Before you came.

ZALMOX

No, I can't completely believe it. Well, shall we
move on? There's something more I want you to
see.

THALIA

Is there any point in going on with this?

ZALMOX

Perhaps not. But don't deny me my chance to
persuade you.

THALIA
(*Forces a smile*)
All right. But I think you're wasting your time.

28 CAMERA TRACKS THALIA   28
    AND ZALMOX AS THEY
    RESUME WALKING

ZALMOX

May I call you Thalia?

THALIA

No.

FADE OUT.

END OF ACT I

ACT TWO

FADE IN:

29 FAÇADE OF LIVING   29
   QUARTERS (STOCK)

30 INT. HALLWAY, DOOR —   30
   THALIA, ZALMOX

                    THALIA
Adelbert lives here?

                    ZALMOX
Yes. Have you ever been inside?

                    THALIA
No, I don't think so. Wait a minute, Zalmox — I'm
not going in while Bert isn't here.

                    ZALMOX
No need to. You can see from here.

                    THALIA
But —

31 CLOSE ANGLE ON DOOR   31

*Zalmox activates the door, which opens to reveal a
room in a shambles.*

32 ANGLE ON THALIA,   32
    ZALMOX LOOKING THROUGH DOOR

THALIA

What . . . has someone searched his quarters?

ZALMOX

No, this is the way he lives.
(*Laughs*)
What glorious disarray!

THALIA

He lives like this? All the time?

ZALMOX

All the time. That prissy-fussy, meticulous man
lives in a pig pen.

THALIA

Well. This is quite a surprise.

ZALMOX

It shouldn't be. Even the most disciplined human
being has an undisciplined side to him.

THALIA

I've never denied that. I simply maintain that it can
be controlled.

ZALMOX

It needs to be acknowledged.

THALIA

We acknowledge it *by* controlling it. Bert has a
slovenly streak — all right. He lets it out here, in the
privacy of his own quarters, where it won't hurt
anything. That's his privilege. And it's his way of
controlling it — he allows it to run rampant here

instead of where it could hurt. In his work. In his own mind.

ZALMOX
You're very quick with an explanation, Dr. Boyd.

THALIA
Let's go. I don't like this.

33 CLOSE ANGLE ON DOOR   33

Zalmox activates the closing mechanism, as we

DISSOLVE TO:

34 TRANSITIONAL SHOT —   34
    MOUNTAIN, DAY (STOCK)

35 MOUNTAIN GLADE, DAY   35

A group of seven or eight persons is picnicking on the mountain side. They are laughing, drinking, obviously having a good time. Camera dollies to couple slightly apart from the others, locked in a tight embrace.

CUT TO:

36 TWO SHOT — THALIA, ZALMOX   36

THALIA
Ah, yes. Is it time for the orgy to begin?

ZALMOX
Would you like to see an orgy?

37 WIDER ANGLE TO   37
    INCLUDE A FEW
    OF THE PICNICKERS

Thalia doesn't answer Zalmox, but moves toward a
GIRL who is on her knees rummaging through a
food container.

THALIA

Hello, Masha.

GIRL
(Startled)
Oh! Oh, hello, Dr. Boyd. And Zalmox!
(Stands)
I didn't see you come up.

THALIA

No.

GIRL
Uh. I didn't hear you, either.

THALIA
Having a good time?

GIRL
Oh, yes. Uh. Yes.

ZALMOX
We were wondering if you could spare a little wine,
Masha. That's a thirsty climb.

GIRL
(Relieved)
Oh, certainly!
(She takes a bottle out of the food container)
Here, take this one. The cork's already loosened.

THALIA
(Dryly)
Sure you can spare it?

> GIRL

Oh, yes. We always bring more than...I
mean...uh. Yes.

> ZALMOX

Thank you, Masha. Enjoy yourself.

> GIRL
> (*Modestly*)

I'll try.
> (*Thalia snorts and moves out of the shot*)

Oh, dear!

> ZALMOX

Don't worry, little one. It's all right.
> (*They exchange a quick hug*)

I'll probably be back later.
> (*He leaves*)

CUT TO:

38   EXT. ANOTHER PLACE   38
ON THE MOUNTAIN, DAY —
THALIA, ZALMOX

*Thalia is leaning against a boulder; Zalmox walks
into the shot and sits on a rock near her. He pulls
the cork out of the bottle and holds the bottle out.*

> ZALMOX

Wine?
> (*When she shakes her head, he takes a drink*)

Ah.
> (*He takes another*)

Why did little Masha irritate you?

> THALIA

"Little Masha" has been taking far too many

picnics lately. She's supposed to be working here,
you know.

ZALMOX

How long has she been on Pythia?

THALIA

About twenty-five years. She was decanted as part
of a control group and then trained as a hematolo-
gist.

ZALMOX

So after twenty-five years perhaps she deserves a
little vacation?

THALIA
(Irritated)

Oh, for heaven's sake, Zalmox! You make Pythia
sound like a slave camp. She's had more freedom
here than she ever would've had on Earth, and a
better education as well. "Little Masha" has never
been in danger of dying from overwork. Most of her
life has been a vacation; she's never contributed
much.

ZALMOX

Just the same, if Pythia is all she knows, perhaps she
deserves a vacation from Pythia.

THALIA

It doesn't really matter. She'll be going to Earth on
the next ship.

39   CLOSE ANGLE ON ZALMOX   39

*He looks at Thalia a moment, and then takes one
last drink. He puts the bottle down and stands up.
Camera follows as he walks over to stand behind
Thalia. Slowly but positively he places his hands on
her breasts.*

THALIA

Take your hands away.
*(He does. She turns to look at him, not angry,
only mildly surprised by what has happened)*
You think I am available to anyone who happens to
wander by?

ZALMOX

No, of course not.

THALIA

Then where did you get the idea that you could
handle my body?

ZALMOX

I was hoping it would be pleasurable for both of us.

THALIA

Then you made a mistake, didn't you?
(No answer)
No, I'm the one who made the mistake. I should
never have come on this fool's errand.

ZALMOX

Are you sure you want to do this?

THALIA

Do what?

ZALMOX

Reject me.
(She looks surprised, and then laughs out loud)
Stop fighting me. Join me.

THALIA

(A beat)
Why don't you stay here and play with the other
children, Zalmox? I have work to do.
(She turns her back on him and walks out)

40 CLOSE ANGLE ON ZALMOX   40

He doesn't move; he is not smiling.

FADE OUT.

END OF ACT II

TAG

41 INT. THALIA BOYD'S 41
OFFICE

*Thalia is reading something in the small viewer on
her desk, drumming her fingers. She seems to have
trouble concentrating. She stands up abruptly and
punches out a number on the large televiewer.*

42 VIEWING SCREEN — 42
TECHNICIAN

TECHNICIAN
Can I help you, Dr. Boyd?

43 WIDER ANGLE TO 43
INCLUDE THALIA LOOKING
AT SCREEN

THALIA
You can tell me what's wrong with Dan.

TECHNICIAN
There's nothing really *wrong* with him, Dr. Boyd.
It's just that he's been making some unusual
demands lately.

THALIA
Like what?

TECHNICIAN
I don't know first-hand; I've just heard some of the
others talking.

THALIA
Is Dr. Tirsos there?

TECHNICIAN
Yes, he's with Dan now.

THALIA
Tell him I want to talk to him.

TECHNICIAN
Just a moment.

44 ANGLE ON THALIA   44

*Camera dollies after Thalia as she walks around the
room, impatiently waiting for Dr. Tirsos.*

45 VIEWING SCREEN — DR. TIRSOS   45

DR. TIRSOS
Thalia!

46 WIDER ANGLE   46

Thalia walks into the shot and faces the screen.

THALIA
Well?

DR. TIRSOS
Dan.

THALIA
Yes? What about Dan?

                    DR. TIRSOS
Are you ready for this one?

                    THALIA
                  (Wondering)
I think so.

                    DR. TIRSOS
Dan wants us to give him a penis.

47   CLOSE ANGLE ON THALIA,   47
     OPEN-MOUTHED.

                              FADE OUT.
                  END

"Well?" asked Jennie. "How did your *scène à faire* go?"

"Predictably," said Zalmox.

"I don't think it's wise, Thalia," said Dr. Tirsos.

"Probably not, but it's less *un*wise than letting this go on." New worry lines had appeared in Thalia's face, caused by the almost complete relaxation of the discipline that had shaped and directed Pythia since its inception. The colony hadn't done a total about-face, but nearly so. Many Pythians no longer even went through the gestures of working.

"Dr. Tirsos is right," offered Dan.

"Don't argue with me, Dan, please. Broadcast my order."

Her order said, in effect, stop screwing around and get back to work. It was the only time in her life she had issued such an order.

Thalia and Dr. Tirsos sat watching the viewscreen in her office to see the Pythians' response. Any direct action resulting from her order was not visible to the naked eye. The Pythians made no defiant moves when Dan's voice informed them playtime was over; they just couldn't be bothered hearing him. The direct order of the head of Pythia Medical Research Project had no effect at all.

"No go," said Dan. "They just aren't listening."

"Pan around, Dan. I want to see what they're doing."

Dan switched the image on the viewscreen to inside the Omph. The place was crowded with noisy, laughing drinkers. Bert was standing on a table delivering a lecture on the evils of continence. Much of the talk was bawdy.

"Saturday night in Podunk Corner," murmured Thalia.

The picture changed, and most of what they saw next was quite different from the boisterous Omph gang. Time after time Dan showed them groups of people just sitting together peacefully, not even talking.

Thalia's door opened to admit Jennie.

"You come to tell me how ill-advised my order was?" Thalia asked wryly.

"No. I thought you might be feeling lonely along about now. I didn't know Dr. Tirsos was here."

Thalia smiled sadly and waved her to a chair. The screen was now showing Zalmox inspecting the fruit that would be ready to pick in three or four days. He was followed by a group of people that ebbed and flowed around him. His height made the Pythians look up every time they spoke to him, but he managed never to look down on them when he answered. Tall, powerful, beautiful Zalmox—clearly the new leader of Pythia.

Jennie thought:

—He is self-transcendence. He does not exist within our limits of good and evil, male and female, child and adult. Union with him is an affirmation of familial ties with all my brothers, all my sisters. The imperative individualism we have been taught breaks down into nothing more than self-adoration. Why worship the chains that imprison one? He is the democratizer *par excellence*. He liberates us from our puny man-made contrivances, our feeble attempts to shape our natures into something they are not. What a relief to be free of all that! To stop posing, to stop playing roles, simply to *be*—without fear of exposure or reprisal! To acknowledge, openly, at last, without fear, that we are what we are. Why *did* Orpheus look back over his shoulder at Eurydice? Art, medicine, social institutions—flimsy disguises for that something in us that makes us want to stand outside ourselves, to deny the limitations of the body. Zalmox is a primal, eruptive, elemental passion, not subject to reason. He is fellowship, exhilaration, abandonment. He is wild and lovely, and majestically calm. He offers peace and joy. A new life. No wise person can deny him.

Thalia thought:

—He is autodestruction. He is disengagement from the man-created world. A derealization of that world. He would fuse and confuse until nothing remains. And yet he is a separator: he is antiself. He would have us abrogate form, continuity, civilization. Shall we fall back to the schisms of the twentieth century, when the only permanence was revolution? Shall we be consenting victims of the iconoclastic drive that demands ever the new—which must vanish as soon as it appears? Must we always be imprisoned in the future? Why should only yesterday and tomorrow wear halos? I do not believe metamorphosis is the only permanent condition.

I refuse to settle for an autistic consciousness, skilled in the craft of self-annihilation, babbling an erotic nonlanguage. How cavalierly we treat our own existence—as if it doesn't matter! *It matters*. Zalmox would negate all that. No wise person can accept him.

Dr. Tirsos thought:

—Jennie and Thalia are right.

"Looks like a bigger crop than the first," Dr. Aliotto said.

"Yes, the second growth usually is," said Zalmox. "But the fruit contains more seeds than the first, and often the taste has just a little edge to it. Not really sour—but there is an aftertaste."

"All the more pity Thalia Boyd still has the first growth locked up."

"Oh, this crop will be good—I didn't mean you wouldn't like it. And Dr. Boyd may still change her mind and let us have the other fruit."

Dr. Aliotto laughed dryly. "My experience with Thalia Boyd has been that she's not given to changing her opinion easily."

"She could be more flexible, couldn't she?" smiled Zalmox. "Well, it doesn't really matter. There'll be plenty here for everybody, and enough seeds for a dozen new plantings."

"You can force-grow a crop directly from the fruit seeds?"

"Yes, but it takes a little longer that way." He reached out a hand to stop Dr. Aliotto from picking a piece of the fruit.

"Not yet," he said.

Thalia was passing the Omph when someone came out and called her name. She turned to face the speaker—and froze.

"Good lord!" she said, aghast. "What are you dressed for, a Hallowe'en party?"

"One tires of wearing lab coats all the time," said Dr. Tirsos easily.

Wide-eyed, Thalia stared at his outfit. He had on short trousers she had never seen him wear before; his tunic was

made of the wildest variegated material imaginable. And his
feet were bare. His shriveled, aged legs looked like two none-
too-straight twigs hanging down from his trousers.

"Second childhood?" she asked, deliberately cruel.

"Perhaps," the old man smiled. "Once in a while it's best
to let go, Thalia. Wouldn't hurt you to do the same. Unbend a
little, let the work go for a while."

Then, horrified, she understood. "So Zalmox has got to
you, too," she said slowly.

"I don't know what you mean by 'got to' me. I think he's
right when he says we're all too work-oriented. Besides, a
little holiday once in a while is bound to be beneficial in the
long run."

A little holiday. Thalia leaned against the Omph doorway
so abruptly that Dr. Tirsos was afraid she was ill. She waved
him away impatiently, and after she had collected her
thoughts, said: "You were the one person on this planet I was
counting on not to give in. I thought surely you could see
through him."

"I can *see* him," answered Dr. Tirsos slowly. "I see that he
has eased our tensions, lessened the strain that has been
building up for years now. I think he is what we need,
Thalia."

"But what's happened to our discipline? How many
experiments have been abandoned half-finished since that
alien arrived? Has everyone forgotten what we're here for?
And you—you, of all people! You've become almost a
symbol of what Pythia exists for—and you abandon all that
to dance to a tune played by some space piper we know
nothing about? What's happened to scientific inquiry,
detachment, objectivity? Is it all so fragile that it collapses the
first time it's tested?"

Just then two of the Briles clone ran by, eyes dancing.
They blew Thalia a kiss.

"And what about that?" Dr. Tirsos asked quietly. "Those
girls have shown you nothing but thinly veiled contempt for
over a year. But that's all in the past now. They feel nothing
but a kind of affectionate fellowship—for everybody. You
have Zalmox to thank for that. Perhaps he's not so alien as he
seems."

Thalia made no attempt to hide the despair she was feeling. Dr. Tirsos placed his hand gently on her shoulder. "You shouldn't resist so hard, Thalia. You're afraid of him, aren't you?"

Reluctantly, she nodded.

"I thought so. Take an old man's advice, my dear, and force yourself to accept Zalmox."

"*Force* myself?"

"Yes. He's gradually been winning the allegiance of everyone on this planet—beginning with Jennie Geiss, that poor, vulnerable child. He obviously offers them something they need, or none of this would be happening. So even if you loathe Zalmox, stop fighting him, Thalia. It's a battle you can't win."

"Then you *do* see through him," she breathed. "You know he is evil."

"I know no such thing," he corrected gently. "All I know is that he is necessary, and he is here. Fake an enthusiasm if you can't work up a real one."

"Why are you doing this?" (*Fear! Betrayal!*)

"I intend to survive," Dr. Tirsos said simply. "And I want you to survive too."

Thalia stared incredulously at the ridiculous-looking figure next to her. This was Dr. Tirsos, the strict, dignified Dr. Tirsos—the standard-setter on Pythia.

"What a sophist you've become," she murmured. "I wish you a speedy recovery."

"You know, Thalia, there comes a time when heroic resistance degenerates into mere willful stubbornness. Swallow your pride. Stop opposing Zalmox."

Her answer was to turn her back on her old advisor and walk away.

"Read Machiavelli, Thalia," he called after her. "Chapter Eighteen."

Out of habit Thalia followed his advice. Back in her office, she found the automatic communicator not working. She kept poking buttons until she roused Dan enough to tell him what she wanted. Soon the words appeared on the screen:

> *You must know, then, that there are two methods of
> fighting, the one by law, the other by force: the first
> method is that of men, the second of beasts; but as the
> first method is often insufficient, one must have
> recourse to the second. It is therefore necessary for a
> prince to know well how to use both the beast and the
> man. This was covertly taught to rulers by ancient
> writers, who relate how Achilles and many others of
> those ancient princes were given to Chiron the centaur
> to be brought up and educated under his discipline.
> The parable of this semi-animal, semi-human teacher is
> meant to indicate that a prince must know how to use
> both natures, and that the one without the other is not
> durable.*

No, thought Thalia. A thousand times no. We are
reasoning creatures, not beasts. Machiavelli was wrong. *You*
are wrong, Dr. Tirsos.

And somehow Pythia has gone wrong.

On Pythia each of the chimpanzees who worked as a
computer repairman possessed a set of tools that was the
latest in modern design. Jacob loved his tools; sometimes
when he wasn't working he would take them out and handle
them just for the sheer pleasure of their feel.

Now he had them all spread out before him. After sitting
down to think about it, he selected one tool, then another,
then another. When he had what he wanted, he packed them
carefully into a kit which he strapped to his back.

The storage room that contained the stranger's fruit was
sealed with a lock that was deactivated by the insertion into a
slot of a punch-coded strip of metal. Dr. Boyd had the metal
strip. But Jacob had his tools.

A close inspection convinced him the slot did not offer the
best way of disengaging the lock. After a brief search he
found a metal panel inset in the wall. No external fixtures of
any kind were visible.

Easy pickings. Jacob had removed this kind of panel
many times.

Once the panel was off, Jacob studied the complicated wiring system carefully. When he was sure he understood it, he opened his tool kit and began to work.

"Get away from there!" Dan's voice boomed out. "Jacob, you know nobody's allowed to monkey with that locking system!"

Jacob worked on.

"All right, I'm yelling for help."

Jacob worked a little faster.

Suddenly the doors hissed and slid open. Jacob helped himself to six pieces of fruit, dumped them into his tool kit, and was gone.

Thalia arrived breathlessly at the animal compound where she found most of Pythia had turned out in answer to Dan's call for help. Nobody wanted to see Jacob hurt. Dan had last spotted the chimp climbing the compound enclosure—and yes, he had eaten some of the fruit.

Pythia was in its night cycle, and Dan, of course, couldn't monitor unlighted areas. Jacob's exact whereabouts were unknown.

"Do we have any spotlights?" Dr. Tirsos asked.

"No time for that." Thalia switched on a control panel. "Dan, find Barry Gomez and tell him to turn on the daylight."

In less than ten minutes Pythia was filled with noon light. Jacob was on the chain-link top of the wolf pen, dropping his tools down through the open spaces on the disturbed and uneasy animals inside. Every time he hit a moving target, he jumped up and down, making that unique chimpanzee noise, half giggle and half grunt. No Pythian chimp who had been taught to communicate through writing had ever been heard to make that noise.

"He's regressed," said Dr. Tirsos. "He's gone back to some primitive ancestral condition. I doubt if he even understands what those men are saying to him."

The men Dr. Tirsos referred to were animal handlers who were trying to coax Jacob down from the top of the pen. Others were vainly trying to calm the restless wolves.

Thalia went over to one of the men. "Why don't you shoot them with tranquillizer darts?"

"No point. These are infected wolves, for testing a new antitoxin. They're carrying an especially virulent strain and tranquillizers don't have any effect on them right now."

"Well, what about Jacob? Can't you tranquillize him?"

"Only with a small, slow-acting dose. A large shot would kill a chimp."

"How slow-acting?"

"Forty-five minutes, an hour."

Thalia moved up to the cage. "Jacob!" she called.

In answer, Jacob hurled a wrench at her. She dodged, and went back to stand by the animal handler. Jacob was using his one remaining tool to cut through the fence-like topping of the pen.

"If he makes a hole in the top," Thalia asked the handler, "will the wolves be able to get out? Can they jump that high?"

"They might," said the man uncertainly. "Some of them are pretty good leapers."

Thalia felt a chill move down her spine. "What have they been infected with?"

"Rabies," said the man.

Oh, pity of god. She looked at the growing circle Jacob was cutting and wanted to cry out in anguish. "You must kill the wolves," she told the handler.

Something like fear appeared in the man's face. "We can't, Dr. Boyd. We don't have rifles or anything like that. We've always controlled the animals by tranquillizing them. Nobody knew this strain of rabies would be resistant until the wolves were already infected. We could gas them, if they were in an enclosed area. But the chimp will have a hole cut in the top before we could drop a shield over the pen."

Thalia and the man stared at each other in dismay as they realized what had to be done. When Thalia found her voice, she told him to get his tranquillizer gun. "And load it with a heavy dosage—the heaviest you've got."

The man looked at her, disturbed, but did as he was told. Thalia's choice: Jacob dead, or rabid wolves loose in Pythia.

The handler had returned, and was waiting to be told specifically what he must do.

The command came: "Shoot Jacob."

Few Pythians heard the "Phtt!" that spelled the end of Jacob's life. But they all saw him jerk upright, place his human hand over his simian face, and plunge head first from the top of the pen. The stunned onlookers stared at the broken body, trying to figure out what had happened.

Thalia turned quickly to the man who had fired. "Do you keep any flammable liquids in the compound?"

"Kerosene. We use it to burn out the pens where diseased animals have been kept."

"Get it. All of it. And hurry."

Thalia called Barry Gomez and told him to put Pythia back on its regular cycle. Night had fully returned when she lighted the first of the kerosene-soaked trees.

Pythians ringed the burning orchard, their faces unreadable in the flickering light of the fire.

"The best thing to do," Zalmox said, "is to go on with our party. Don't dwell on Jacob's death; that will just make you turn inward and won't help anybody. He's dead, and he shouldn't *be* dead—but it's done. Accept it."

"What about your trees?" asked Claude.

Zalmox lifted his shoulders and let them drop.

They were in the Omph. Jennie and Claude and Bert stared at Zalmox glumly. Barry and Cynthia were making a listless attempt at dancing to the insipid music coming from the wall speaker.

Angelina Baker walked in and eased herself into a chair. "Man, you certainly throw a wild party," she said to Zalmox.

"One thing that might help would be some real music," Zalmox said. "You two really getting a kick out of that hormone music?" he called to Barry and Cynthia.

Cynthia shrugged and sat down disconsolately. Barry turned off the music. The silence that seeped in was heavy and oppressive.

Angelina finally spoke. "That's an improvement?"

"How about some Bach?" asked Claude.

"Puccini," said Jennie. "I feel like crying."

"No," said Zalmox. "What we need is something

different." He moved to the control panel and activated it. "Dan, this is Zalmox. I need your help."

"Of course, dear boy. What can I do for you?"

"Play impresario for us. Does Pythia do any monitoring of radio signals from space?"

"You mean do we listen to the Crab Nebula's death rattle and that kind of racket? Heavens, no. We leave all *that* sort of thing to Uraniborg."

"But you are in contact with Uraniborg?"

"Unwaveringly."

"Then you could monitor their reception of a pulsar's signals, couldn't you?"

"I could, but whatever for? Why do you want to record a pulsar's beat?"

"I don't want to record it, I want you to broadcast it over the Omph's speaker system."

"*Over the speaker!*"

"That's right. Try to get CP 0950, in Leo. Have you ever heard it?"

"Well, I did eavesdrop once or twice."

"Then you know it's a foot-tapper. Four beats a second."

"I don't have feet. At least, not functional ones."

"Come on, Dan. Hook us into CP 0950."

"Oh, very well. This will take a while."

But it didn't. Very soon the rapid, stimulating beat of the jazziest pulsar in the galaxy came through the speaker system. Almost unconsciously Cynthia responded to the beat and began to move in time to the rhythm. Jennie and Angelina laughed and began to clap in accompaniment. Cynthia stood up and began to dance.

"That's fine, Dan," said Zalmox. "Now do you think you could tune into the radio waves given off by the hydrogen gas lying along a spiral arm of the galaxy?"

"Any particular arm?"

"Perseus, I think. It has a nice sound."

The Perseus sound had a different pitch and rhythm from that of CP 0950. "Syncopation!" cried Jennie, and jumped up to join Cynthia in her dance.

"Dan—"

"Nope. My turn." Dan was getting into his role of

impresario. "Try this."

"This" had a longer pulse length than either of the other two sounds. It also varied its pitch from beat to beat. In combination with the Leo pulsar and the Perseus arm, it made a catchy little tune.

"Terrific!" cried Zalmox. "What is it?"

"A birth cry," said Dan smugly. "A new star getting itself born. In Orion."

By now Bert was on his feet doing a solo in the center of a circle of laughing, bobbing people. His chubby body bounced up and down and soon sweat began to appear on his face. He laughed and fell back to join the circle. Angelina took his place.

New sounds succeeded each other rapidly. As soon as Dan found a sound he liked, he locked it into the rhythm already going. He was thoroughly enjoying his job of orchestrating the noise of the universe into music.

"It's too confining in here," said Zalmox. "Let's go outside. Dan, can you transfer your sounds to the speakers by the recreation area?"

"Of course," sang Dan.

"Then turn 'em on!" shouted Claude.

"Hell, turn 'em *all* on!" cried Jennie.

They spilled out of the Omph to find the streets of Pythia pulsating with their universal music. Passersby had stopped to smile and tap their feet.

"The mountain!" cried Zalmox.

"The mountain!" cried Cynthia. And turned a cartwheel.

Doors opened and people came out, smiling, to see what was going on. Dr. Aliotto grinned as the party danced past him; he decided to tag along.

"The mountain!" Jennie shouted.

"The mountain!" the others echoed.

HUM diddle diddle diddle HUM diddle HUM diddle HUM diddle diddle diddle HUM.

Claude swept Jennie up in a bear hug and swung her around three or four times before putting her down again. They ran on with the others. There were twenty-five or thirty of them now; more were joining in. Dan was tracking them; each wall speaker sprang into life as they approached it.

Right behind Jennie, Dr. Aliotto laughed and hugged Angelina.

HUM diddle diddle diddle.

The mountainside sang in welcome. Dan had activated all the consoles embedded in the mountain rock, and Zalmox led the dancing, laughing group up the slope.

"Eddie and Matt," he cried out, "where are you?"

"Here!" two high voices answered. Jennie hadn't seen the twins join them.

"Give me a hand," said Zalmox. "What we need is some refreshment." From a small cave opening Zalmox and the two boys dragged out a large container filled with bottles of wine. "The Boy Scouts have nothing on me," Zalmox said. "Jennie, the first one's for you." He tossed a bottle over the heads of five people that stood between them.

Jennie shrieked and almost dropped the bottle. But didn't. Claude pried the cork out, and Jennie took a long swallow to start the drinking party.

HUM diddle HUM diddle HUM diddle diddle diddle HUM.

The bottles were passed around rapidly. More Pythians had joined them as the music seemed to grow louder.

Cynthia and Barry and Sam Flaherty were doing a dance that suggested sex was really a three-person job. Angelina was stretched out on the ground, panting from her exertion. Eddie and Matt were throwing wine corks at her.

"Hey, everybody, look at this!" Dan boomed above the noise.

One of the console screens was showing a scene from somewhere in the park. Dr. Indhara was doing a strip-tease on the grass, performing a clumsy sort of dance to the cosmic beat that throbbed everywhere. He was surrounded by a circle of young girls who were whistling and cheering him on.

"Great idea!" cried Jennie. "Come on Sam, show us how it's done."

"I'm going to show you *all* my webbing," sang Sam in mock-sensuous tones. He did a bump and a grind, and another for good measure. When the crowd roared approval, he began to strip. He was wearing only two garments—a tunic and short trousers. Each piece of clothing was tossed high into the air, and Sam didn't seem too concerned when a ripping sound announced several people had grabbed at the same time. The music was too fast to allow a "teasing" performance, so in no time flat Sam was stark naked.

"Never realized you were that good-lookin', boy," said Angelina from her prone position. Sam immediately tried to stretch out on top of her, but Angelina deftly rolled out of the way—to a chorus of boos and laughter from the onlookers.

Sam scrambled to his feet and slapped Jennie lightly on the shoulder. "Tag," he said. "You're *It*."

Jennie felt arms and hands thrusting her into the center of the circle. She was surrounded by laughing eyes and upturned bottles. Someone held a bottle out to her; she took a swallow and began her dance. She wriggled out of her tunic and tossed it to Claude. Bra next: when she had trouble unfastening it, Eddie ran out to help. Zalmox laughed and grabbed him around the waist, lifting him back to the circle. "It's more fun the way she does it," he told the boy.

Shorts last. A huge cheer rose from the mountain side, and Jennie turned automatically to Claude. But stopped. Unexpectedly she whirled and placed her hand on Dr. Aliotto's shoulder.

"Oh-*ho*!" said the surprised crowd, and no one was more surprised than Dr. Aliotto. But he lumbered to his feet and good-naturedly performed his part in the ritual. Undressed, he looked like a great shambling bear.

"Man, what a gut he's got on him," said Claude. Jennie had already noticed: and was surprised to feel a stirring in her own body at the sight.

Dr. Aliotto had tagged Angelina, and now the big black woman was struggling out of her clothes. "I can't stand it! I can't stand it, I tell you!" Sam was yelling, while Bert and Barry laughingly held him back. Finally Angelina got her clothes off, and she stood there large-boned and heavy. Jennie suspected that every man in the place wanted her.

But it was Cynthia Howell who ran out and threw her arms around the black woman. "You're *gorgeous*, Angelina!" she said.

"I guess that makes you 'It', honey," said Angelina, and yielded stage to the younger woman.

Bra-less Cynthia was out of her clothes in an eyewink, and instead of tagging Barry, she chose Claude. *Claude* chose Barry. Bert complained of being left out, and immediately four pairs of hands helped him undress. That was the signal: the revelers began shedding clothing as if it were contaminated.

"What about Zalmox?" someone cried.

"Way ahead of you," he laughed. He had been standing nude in their midst for some time. Cynthia and a girl Jennie didn't know made a leap for him, and, laughing, he allowed himself to be forced to the ground.

"What are you doing? What do you think you're doing? *Stop it*! STOP IT!"

Jennie realized she had heard this command several times. She turned and saw Thalia Boyd staring at them with revulsion. "Stop it!" Thalia cried. "*What's the matter with you?*"

Little by little the noises stopped. Only the spatial music still pulsed away. The revelers turned toward Thalia resentfully.

"Are you out of your minds?" said Thalia. "Look at you! You've gone completely berserk! Put on your clothes and your sanity and get back to where you belong!" The music stopped.

The silence that followed was broken by the sound of a wine bottle shattering on a rock. Somebody muttered something that sounded ugly. Zalmox and the two girls stood up.

"Stop and think!" Thalia commanded. "Have you lost *all* your judgment? Dr. Baker, Dr. Aliotto, Dr. Billings—put on your clothing and come back with me!"

A wine bottle sailed so close to Thalia's head that she jerked away in astonishment. The bottle shattered behind her.

Jennie stepped up to her quickly. "Instead of our coming back with you," she said, "why don't you stay here with us?"

"Yeah, take off your clothes and stay a while!" someone yelled. The laughter that greeted this had changed its quality somewhat. Not so carefree now.

Thalia whirled on Zalmox. "You must be quite pleased

with yourself! All along this is what you wanted. You came here with the intention of destroying us!"

Cynthia stepped protectively in front of Zalmox. Over her head, Zalmox smiled. "Relax, Dr. Boyd," he said. "Jennie extended you an invitation. I second it. Why don't you join us?"

"Join you?" A look of long-repressed loathing came over Thalia's face. "Never. I'll die before I join *you*."

"Oh, come now, Thalia," interjected Jennie. "Isn't that a little melodramatic? What are you afraid of? We're just having a good time. Or we *were*. Zalmox gave you some good advice. Relax. Here, have a drink." And Jennie held out her wine bottle.

With one sweep of her arm, Thalia knocked the bottle out of Jennie's hand. The bottle fell to the ground without breaking, the red liquid flowing around their feet.

"You silly little birdbrain," snapped Thalia. "The fact that *you're* so easily seduced doesn't mean we all have to be!"

Birdbrain? Easily seduced?

Without saying a word, Jennie reached out and grabbed the neckline of Thalia's jacket. She pulled down, hard. The ripping sound brought a yelp of delight from the crowd.

Thalia looked at Jennie in pain and fright; then, without speaking, she turned and ran.

A shout rose from the crowd. In six strides Zalmox had overtaken Thalia. "Hold her arms, Jennie!" he called. Jennie slipped behind Thalia and grabbed her arms. Many hands assisted Zalmox in undressing Thalia Boyd.

The shouting of the crowd became almost rhythmic. Jennie knelt on the ground, pulling Thalia down from behind so that her head was in Jennie's lap. "Get her, Zalmox," someone muttered. Zalmox dropped to his knees beside the two women.

"You're mad!" Thalia was screaming. "You're *all* mad! Let me go! You don't know what you're doing!"

"Oh, I know what I'm doing," smiled Zalmox. He placed his hands on her knees and forced them apart.

Thalia struggled to get away, but Jennie held on tightly. Thalia looked at Zalmox kneeling over her.

"A bull," she breathed. "You're a bull!"

Zalmox laughed, and thrust home.

The cheering section roared with delight. Jennie laughed. Zalmox laughed. Their heads were close together: he kissed her.

Soon Jennie felt the struggle go out of Thalia's body; the older woman lay inert under Zalmox's ministrations. Jennie relaxed her hold. She looked at the other woman's body, heaving under Zalmox. Jennie reached out her hands and cupped Thalia's breasts. So soft, so nice. She leaned over and kissed Thalia's mouth.

When she lifted her head, she was surprised to see Dr. Aliotto where Zalmox had been. Zalmox was sitting nearby, watching and laughing.

When Dr. Aliotto was finished, Barry fell on Thalia with such force that he knocked Jennie away. She rolled over to Zalmox, and saw he still had an erection. She put her hand between his legs.

"Certainly," he said, and pulled her on top of him.

Sitting astride Zalmox, Jennie saw Sam Flaherty at last getting his wish: he was pumping away at Angelina Baker with a look of utter ecstasy on his face. Bert was now on top of Thalia, while Dr. Aliotto sat nearby. Waiting for seconds.

Cynthia was showing Eddie and Matt how.

Zalmox gave Jennie a final thrust that sent her laughing into the air. She came down to find a Briles girl taking her place. Claude seemed to be busy with another of the Briles girls at the moment, so Jennie went over to wait until Dr. Aliotto had finished his second bout with Thalia.

"Have a heart, Jennie," he said when she pulled him toward her. "I need *some* recovery time."

"Nonsense. Climb aboard."

Dr. Aliotto found he had more staying power than he thought.

Jennie had trouble standing up. Too much wine. Or something. She tried to focus her eyes enough to identify the man lying on top of Thalia. It was Charlie, the balding man from Central Control.

She stumbled and fell. Just as she had gotten to her hands and knees, she felt the weight of a body on her back.

"Promise me you'll always stay just the way you are," said a familiar voice.

"Barry?" Jennie twisted her head around to see.

"Right," he grinned. He grasped her hips and worked his way in from behind. She held herself open and still, letting him do all the work. When they had spent themselves, he kissed the back of her neck. The way he used to do.

"Hey, Barry, can I take a ride?" called Sam Flaherty.

"Sure," laughed Barry, yielding his place to Sam. "Why not?"

"Ask *me*," said Jennie.

"Okay. Hey, Jennie, can I take a ride? Can I? Huh?"

"It seems you already are 'taking a ride,' " she said, not displeased.

Sam rode her hard, and before long they were both exhausted. Sam finally pulled himself to his feet, and Jennie heard Bert ask, "Me next?"

"Oh, Bert," she said, "my knees hurt."

"You saying no?"

"Nope. I'm saying my knees hurt." She rolled over on her back and lifted her legs.

Bert came almost immediately. "Sorry," he apologized.

" 'S okay."

Bert moved away and Eddie plopped down between her legs. "Is it all right if I call you Jocasta?" he asked.

Jennie laughed, first in amusement and then in delight at how much the boy had learned so quickly. When they had both climaxed, Eddie lay completely relaxed on top of her, breathing deeply, perspiring. She eased him gently off to the side, and once again struggled to her feet.

This time she walked slowly and very carefully. Figures were lying everywhere, in various states of exhaustion. Sam Flaherty was on Thalia. Jennie came upon Claude uncorking a new bottle, and she settled herself beside him.

"I just had Angelina Baker," he said.

"Oh?" said Jennie, interested. "How was it?"

"Rather overwhelming," he laughed, handing her the bottle. Good wine. They curled up together to watch the others.

Zalmox walked by with several bottles under his arms. "Everything all right here?"

The perfect host.

Dr. Aliotto and Angelina Baker were lying side by side, breathing heavily.

Jennie glanced over to where Thalia was lying. A man got up; another kneeled down.

"That reminds me," said Claude. "I haven't had my turn at Thalia yet."

"Then you'd better hurry," said Jennie. "I don't know if she'll last much longer."

"I don't know if *I*'ll last much longer," he said as he left.

Jennie sipped at the wine, feeling more relaxed than she could remember ever having felt before. A warm drowsiness took hold, and she was only vaguely aware of Zalmox bending over to stroke her cheek. Through half-closed eyes she watched him walk away.

Beautiful butt.

She was just starting to drift off when she felt herself covered by a body—ah, yes, a very male body. Jennie wondered whose body it was. All she had to do to find out was open her eyes.

Her eyes stayed closed.

Jennie was smiling as he began to make love to her. He took his time, and Jennie was in no hurry. When he was finished, her unseen lover kissed both her breasts and left. She immediately fell asleep.

"How 'bout sharin' the joy juice, honey?" a low voice roused her.

Jennie looked over to see Angelina lying near her. "How can you drink it lying down?"

"I'll find a way," said Angelina. "Just pass it over."

Jennie handed her the bottle and watched as Angelina tilted it in the air and aimed the red stream for her mouth. Some of it found the target.

"Claude says you're kind of overwhelming," said Jennie.

"Claude?" Angelina sounded puzzled. "You mean Claude Billings? Was he here too?"

Jennie laughed and patted Angelina's arm.

Bert, followed by Eddie and Matt, placed two bottles of

wine on the ground and sat down. "Zalmox sent these," he said. "He was feeling sorry for you two lonely, neglected women."

Eddie and Matt took on the job of opening the bottles, which they did with a certain élan.

"How was your rite of passage, boys?" Angelina asked. "Enjoy it?"

"You bet!" said Eddie enthusiastically. "And it's about time, too. I was getting so tired of just *reading* about fucking."

Angelina snored.

"Hey!" said Eddie, prodding her with his foot. "You can't go to sleep now."

Angelina lifted her head. "Why the hell not?"

"Uh, I don't know why not. But you can't."

"He's right, Angelina," said Barry, coming up with Cynthia. "You can't go to sleep."

"Will you marry me?" Matt asked Cynthia.

"Not right now," she said, "but I will have some of your wine."

Zalmox was there again, passing out bottles.

Claude was back. "Not exactly a live one, is she?"

That looked like Dr. Indhara having a go at Thalia. Evidently the party on the mountainside was better than the one in the park.

Barry's cloud hovered overhead. Its creator heaved an empty wine bottle at it—missing, of course.

Dr. Aliotto was hefting a rock in his hand. "What Pythia needs," he said, "is a major league ball team." And he threw a sliding curve at the nearest console. The screen shattered into a thousand fragments.

They all laughed. What a funny thing to do.

Claude's pagemaster bleeped. (Someone still on duty?) Claude ripped the pagemaster off his wrist and smashed it between two rocks as if it were an insect. Another funny.

Matt went over to Thalia.

"Wanna foal lie," mumbled Angelina.

"You wanna *what*?" laughed Bert.

"Fo-al lie. Wanna foal lie."

"Foal lie. You don't mean *vocalize*, do you?"

"Yeah. Voal lie."

"Good idea," said Jennie. "A *Singspiel*."

"But no counterpoint," said Sam Flaherty.

"Or any kind of point," said Jennie.

DAS SINGSPIEL AUF DEM BERGE

1. *Phallacious reasoning*
Said Angelina: The Chinese discovered the directive property of the magnetic needle but didn't know what to do with it. It was Arab sailors who came along and put the needle in a compass and used it for navigation. Did you know I'm really Arabian?

2. *Toujours l'amour toujours*
Said Claude: I'm in love with two synthetic girls, Polly and Esther. I was trying to choose between them when they informed me they preferred not to be separated. Not even for me. But I was welcome to link on to their chain, if I so desired. I so desired.

3. *Outrée entrée*
Said Dr. Aliotto: I don't like Italian food, even though my father's mother came from Naples. When I was small I asked her what Chicken Tetrazzini was; she said a chicken with four zinis. I immediately put myself on a diet of Cream of Wheat flambé.

4. *Vaya con frijoles*
Said Jennie: There's an old poem that asks an overwhelming question, "ποῦ μοι τὰ καλὰ δέλῖνα";—which means "Where is my beautiful parsley?" Sounds lovely in Greek, but how do you work it into a conversation?

5. *Drang und Sturm*

Said Bert: I always seem to get things backward. I once lowered eyebrows at a wedding reception where I shook hands with the bride and kissed the groom. Ah, well. Time wounds all heels.

6. *No matter how hard she practices, she'll never be a tenor*

Sang Eddie and Matt: Yes! We have no sopranos; we have no sopranos today! We've tenors, contraltos, and baritones—snare drums, and fiddles, and saxophones. But yes! We have no sopranos; we have no sopranos today!

7. *Under the rainbow*

Said Cynthia: Not possessing the kind of vision that can penetrate Kryptonite, I have often wondered why the off-color color is "blue." Why can't a risqué story be orange? Or magenta? Tell me a dirty joke in surprise pink. Or bastard amber.

8. *Persiflage in a prison*

Said Sam Flaherty: Playfully pummeling pillows, Peter Piper presented his plea: "I hate pickled peppers. I always have hated them. But if there's anything I hate more than pickled peppers, it's pecking them. I mean picking. Perhaps you have perceived a peculiar propensity in me," he said. "I perpetuate the pattern. There's a positive purpose propelling me—pushing, persuading, prolonging my problem." He pinched a plump persimmon, patted his panting pekinese, and plopped down at the player piano. "I hate it," said Peter. Peevishly.

9. *A spider doing push-ups on a mirror*

Said Barry: We've become too sophisticated for our own good. We need to get back to fundamentals, and ain't that an original thought. Do away with decimal fractions and go back to sexagesimal fractions. Do away with logarithms and go back to prosthaphaeresis. Do away with weather and go back to nonweather. Do away with.

10. *Un rêve bien fait*
Said Jennie: I dreamed that Aeschylus was a high priest,
performing a ritual ceremony in the temple. Euripides
marched up and down the street in front of the temple,
carrying a protest sign. Down at the end of the street stood
Sophocles, watching them both, smiling and shaking his
head.

11. *Help save the cherry orchard*
Said Dr. Aliotto: I want to thank you all for your unwavering
support during my period of "disgrace" on the only planet in
the galaxy (that we know of) dedicated solely to medical
research. I am fully cognizant of my responsibility to uphold
the highest scientific standards possible at all times. At ease,
disease: fungus among us, malaria in the area.

12. *Beware the Jubjub bird*
Said Claude: Doesn't the orderliness of things sometimes
make you *sick*? Keep them there cycles rolling: carbon,
autobone, self-calcification. Full fathom five thy future lies;
of such groans are morals made.

13. *The first stone*
Said Sam: When Snaking Day was first celebrated in Eden,
reactions were a bit mixed. Adam was a have-your-cake-and-
eat-it-too kind of guy; so when the party got rough, he
quickly passed the buck to Eve. Ever since then, Eve has
preferred the buck to Adam.

14. *Camus to you, too*
Said Eddie: Take a simple sentence: The boy threw the ball.
Subject, verb, direct object. Now substitute words—'horse'
for 'boy', 'shuffled' for 'threw', 'pancakes' for 'ball'. The horse
shuffled the pancakes. Subject, verb, direct object. Gram-
matically impeccable. For sixty-four scillion dollars: why
can't pattern function independently of content?

15. *Newton doesn't live here any more*
Said Angelina: I think I ought to tell you the rate of circulation of the blood is slowing down. Cause: traffic congestion. Drugs, additives, you name it—they're clogging up the arteries and the veins and the capillaries and causing the blood to flow more and more slowly until one day it's going to stop altogether. Honest.

16. *Nine reasons why I suspect thee*
Said Jennie: Hieronymo was perfectly sane; just he and me—never thee. The two of us sat down one day and talked it out. You don't believe in ghosts. Pity. We decided to consult an expert; and since he couldn't come to us, we went to Elsinore. Result: a fiction-finding committee. You come too, they said, we need a choral voice. (I muttered under my breath, but in the end kept quiet.) First we petitioned Hera to see if she could whip her boy back into shape again; she could, and we had might on our side. For insurance, we decided a little right wouldn't hurt, so we enlisted Galahad to the cause. We had a big argument over Medea, but finally agreed we couldn't afford to pass up anyone with a dragon-drawn chariot at her disposal. The Daughter of Indra didn't receive a single vote; relieved, we welcomed Porphyro in her stead. Cleopatra for speed and Prospero for ballast, and we were ready to begin our flight to the moon for a quick game with Marianne Moore's ball club. The Lunar League won.

17. *Lions and tigers and bears—oh my!*
Said Matt: Does an errant parent always produce a wild child? My brother and I were once united, but then someone gave the order to separate us. Who decided that?

18. *Ramadan days*
Said Barry: We so often listen to the wrong voice. Ptolemy instead of Aristarchus. Paracelsus instead of Agricola. Bateman instead of Kammerer. And the wolf has his foot in the door again.

19. *Yondah is my faddah's palace*
Said Cynthia: Shall we acronymicize? Pythia: Society for the Cure of All Bodily Sickness. SCABS. Physician, peel thyself.

20. *Peel your own grape*
Said Bert: Fuck you. Up yours. Uh:.. go screw yourself. Anything else? Well, I guess you get the idea.

21. *Have a bob of cherries*
Said Jennie: Your trouble is you could never believe in the miracle of midwinter fertility. You may think you are half in love with easeful death. And perhaps you are: but *I* am Duchess of Malfi still.

22. *My dog has fleas*
Sang Pythia: The broadbacked figure drest in blue and green enchanted the maytime with an antique flute like a lame balloonman's whistle

far

and

wee

TAAAAAAAAAAAAAAAAAAAAA

DZEEEEEEEEEEEEEEEE

OOOOOOOOOOOOOOO

23. *Now could I drink hot blood, and do such bitter business as the day would quake to look on*
Said Zalmox: Have some fruit.

Part III

Cadmus.

                                   Enough. No more.
When you realize the horror you have done,
you shall suffer terribly. But if with luck
your present madness last until you die,
you will seem to have, not having, happiness.

Agave.

Why do you reproach me? Is there something wrong?

Cadmus.

First raise your eyes to the heavens.

Agave.

                                       There.
But why?

Cadmus.

                      Does it look the same as it did before?
Or has it changed?

Agave.

                      It seems—somehow—clearer,
brighter than it was before.

Cadmus.

                            Do you still feel
the same flurry inside you?

Agave.

                            The same—flurry?
No, I feel—somehow—calmer. I feel as though—
my mind were somehow—changing.

                                  —*Euripides*
                                  The Bacchae

Pain. *Pain, pain, pain.*

And darkness.

Jennie realized her eyes had been open for several minutes—and she could see nothing.

Her head throbbed, her eyes stung, the back of her neck felt as if someone had been pounding on it.

And she could see nothing.

She didn't know where she was. She fought down a feeling of panic and began to feel around her. Loose dirt. Not inside a building, then. A few more minutes of this and she at last found her voice. "Hello? Anybody? I can't see! Hello?"

"Is that you, Jennie?" a voice answered. "Hold on. I'm putting a new power pack in my hand lamp; the old one just fizzled out. We'll have some light in a minute."

She thought two things simultaneously: *I'm not blind* and *It's Dr. Tirsos.* A light flashed out, and the beam played over the ground until it located her. Jennie covered her eyes, and Dr. Tirsos lowered the light.

"Are you all right?" he was asking her.

"I never felt worse in my life. What happened? What time is it?"

"It's almost noon."

"Noon!" In her surprise, Jennie didn't notice her first question went unanswered. "Then why is it so dark?"

"All the power has gone off. *All* of it. The emergency power system failed to cut in; I've been trying to activate it manually, but I can't do it alone. Can you walk, Jennie? I need help."

Just then the beam of Dr. Tirsos's hand lamp caught a figure lying on the ground nearby, breathing heavily—Claude Billings. Jennie tried to wake him. No response. He lay like a leaden thing, impervious to Jennie's attempt to rouse him.

"What's wrong with him? Why is he sleeping like that?"

"Lights first, Jennie. Then clean-up."

Clean-up?

She used Dr. Tirsos's hand to help pull herself to her feet. She stumbled and experienced a moment of dizziness—Dr. Tirsos's light was all she had to orient herself to.

"Take hold of my arm," Dr. Tirsos said, "and watch where you're stepping."

She kept her eyes on the ground circled by the beam from the lamp, and almost immediately they were walking over broken glass—large jagged fragments of it. They had to go slowly because of Jennie's bare feet, which were already bleeding. They detoured around some spilled liquid that was giving off wisps of steam. Jennie uttered a small cry when they came upon Eddie asleep in his own vomit.

"Keep going," said Dr. Tirsos grimly.

They reached a stilled moveway which they followed to the center of the colony. They passed communication panels which had been torn forcibly from the walls, more broken glass, machines which had been smashed beyond recognizability. And everywhere among the debris were sprawled naked, drunken figures—sleeping it off.

The sour odor over everything made Jennie gag. She pulled away from Dr. Tirsos long enough to empty her queasy stomach.

No sooner had she finished than Dr. Tirsos said, "Please, Jennie, we must hurry. I've been hunting for someone who was conscious; you're the first to wake up. If we don't activate the emergency power system soon, we're going to run out of breathable air. Don't you understand, Jennie? Our life-support system has broken down."

Then it hit her. "Dan!"

"Yes. Something has happened to Dan. Come on."

She forced herself to hurry. Dr. Tirsos led her into a building and then down long flights of stairs (the drop shafts weren't working).

"Why is it so far underground?" she asked.

"To protect it from unexpected catastrophe," he said dryly. "Here we are."

"How do we activate it? How complicated is it?"

"Not complicated at all. Just pull one big old-fashioned switch."

"Then why—"

Dr. Tirsos sighed. "I'm an old man, Jennie, and not very strong. I couldn't manage it by myself."

Jennie soon saw why. The switch was heavy and stiff, and the two of them pulling together couldn't budge it. It was only when Jennie threw her entire weight on the top of the switch that it groaned and moved down to the *ON* position. Jennie tumbled to the floor and the emergency power system hummed into life.

The lights came on, and for the first time Jennie became fully aware of her own nakedness. Without saying a word, Dr. Tirsos took off his lab coat and handed it to her. She felt vaguely ashamed as she slipped it on.

The shame became less vague as they climbed the stairs to the surface. Jennie walked more and more slowly as detail after detail of last night's madness forced its way into her conscious acknowledgment. All those men . . . and Thalia! My god—*Thalia.* At the top of the stairs she stopped.

Dr. Tirsos seemed to understand what was happening. "You are going to have to face it, my dear," he said gently. And opened the door.

The stench hit them hard. Even granite-faced Dr. Tirsos showed signs of queasiness. In the light they saw disorder rampant—smashed equipment, broken wine bottles, clothing strewn everywhere, food dumped among the glass fragments. And here and there among the debris, a sleeping Pythian. Unknowing and uncaring.

"Look," said Dr. Tirsos.

At their feet lay a goat, its throat cut.

For the second time in half an hour, Jennie vomited.

Dr. Tirsos barely waited for her to finish before he said "Dan" and started to walk away. Jennie stumbled after him, dizzy and still gagging.

"What is it?" she asked. "What's causing that nauseating odor?"

"The body-parts bank," he answered. "The refrigeration has been off long enough for the parts to have thawed out. Some of the organs are beginning to decompose."

Jennie kept her eyes on the ground as she trudged along after Dr. Tirsos. She wasn't ready for this, not yet.

At the entrance to Dan's building, Dr. Tirsos stopped. "Before we go in, Jennie," he said, "you must understand that Dan doesn't exist any more. I could see well enough by my hand lamp to determine that his brain had been torn out of its casing. What we're going in for is to estimate what's needed for repair."

Jennie stared at him blankly. "Dan doesn't exist any more?"

"He's dead, Jennie," said the old man firmly. "Now, come on."

Inside, she leaned helplessly against the wall as Dr. Tirsos tried to make his way through the jumble of wires and parts that had once supported Dan's life. Had supported all their lives. Her shock was so great that she stared at a lump of gray matter on the floor for a full minute before she recognized it as a human brain.

Dr. Tirsos came back to her carrying a small oxygen tank. "Jennie, I want you to take this and go out and rouse as many people as you can. I need—Jennie! Listen to me!"

Jennie stared at him glassy-eyed.

"Jennie, you must concentrate! You're all the help I have."

She forced herself to focus on the worried old face in front of her.

"Now listen. You've got to organize a work crew. Get them on their feet and suited up. Those decomposing parts must be hauled outside the shield and dumped into the nearest ravine. The emergency waste converter isn't equipped to handle that big a load. Do you understand?"

She nodded dumbly.

"And every time you find someone who worked on Dan, send him here. All the life-support systems are damaged, as far as I can tell; I want to see if I can construct one complete system from the undamaged parts. But in order to do that, I need help, *lots* of help. Do you understand *that*?"

"Yes."

"And one more thing," said Dr. Tirsos. "Find Thalia."

• • •

Find Thalia.

Outside, Jennie forced herself to lift her eyes and look at Pythia. The destruction was overwhelming.

—*Thalia, Thalia*!

Woodenly she moved among the sleepers. She knelt by a technician, the one Dan had once chewed out for careless footwork, and applied the oxygen mask. As soon as he was sufficiently awake to understand what she was saying, she sent him to Dr. Tirsos.

After Jennie had aroused six more sleepers and explained what needed to be done about the decomposing body parts, she turned her steps toward the mountain. Find Thalia, Dr. Tirsos had said. But Zalmox is the one I want to find, she thought.

And when I find him, I'm going to kill him.

The mountain. Yesterday's pleasure spot, today's obscenity. Claude was still sleeping leadenly as she'd left him. Matt was sleeping in Sam Flaherty's arms. Old Mrs. Indhara slept with her hand on Barry Gomez's genitals. A girl of eleven or twelve slept with the neck of a wine bottle inserted in her vagina. Angelina Baker was snoring, one leg flung over Dr. Aliotto—who, Jennie saw, was awake and staring around him in horror.

Silently she knelt beside him and offered the oxygen mask. He took several deep whiffs without looking at her. "Dr. Tirsos needs all the cyberneticists who can walk," she told him, "to help repair . . . to help build a new cyborg. Will you take care of that?"

Dr. Aliotto nodded without speaking, stood up, looked around for a pair of trousers, and shambled away.

"Jennie?"

The voice was weak, but Jennie recognized it. "Take some oxygen, Bert. It helps."

The pharmacist breathed deeply, the mask clasped to his mouth and nose. He and Jennie avoided each other's eyes.

"Is it . . . is it as bad as it looks?" he finally asked.

"Dan has been destroyed and we're on the emergency support system. Pythia is a shambles."

Bert turned his head away and vomited. Jennie watched dispassionately.

"As soon as you're able," she said, "go to the body-parts bank. Help is needed."

Bert struggled to his feet and began to stumble away.

"And pick up an environmental suit on your way," she called to his retreating back. He raised a hand in acknowledgment.

Jennie felt a light touch on her arm and turned to see the distraught face of Cynthia Howell peering over her shoulder. "What can I do?" the girl asked.

"Find Thalia," said Jennie. Cynthia nodded and moved away.

—*Please* find her, thought Jennie. I can't. I can't.

She worked automatically now. Wake them up, explain. Claude, Barry, the Indharas, the child violated by the wine bottle, Angelina, Charlie, What's-his-Name, Eddie, four of the Briles clone, somebody else, somebody else. When she woke Sam and Matt, the two had stared at each other in revulsion. Then the twin had burst into tears. Jennie dropped the oxygen tank and put her arms around the boy.

Before long the mountainside was a mass of groaning, retching, wretched people. No one questioned Jennie when she instructed them to go either to the body-parts bank or to Dr. Tirsos. They seemed grateful to be told what to do.

The light touch on Jennie's arm again, but this time the girl's face was as old as Maya Indhara's.

"I found Thalia," Cynthia said. "She's dead."

Jennie joined her fellow-murderers in the stomach-turning job of carrying out the decaying body parts. Like the others, she quickly learned to wear her environmental suit inside the shield as well as outside. The air in the body-parts bank was unbreathable. She also learned they had been asleep for nearly forty hours, not just overnight. Some of the organs had decayed to the point they had to be sucked up by hand vacuums. Then the vacuums had to be thrown into the ravine.

The Pythians worked silently, each caught in his own

memories. Claude Billings remembered standing on the observation platform and urinating on Dan, and then prying a protesting speaker out of the wall to hurl at one of Dan's monitoring eyes. Barry Gomez remembered tightening a rope around his own neck until he got an erection. Angelina Baker remembered slaughtering a sheep and pouring its steaming blood over Dan's new spleen. Adelbert Phillips remembered defecating on the computer terminal in the pharmacy. Cynthia Howell remembered letting Bert's donkey mount her. Joseph Aliotto remembered turning the pathology lab ovens on to full, disengaging the safety valves, and calmly watching as the ovens burned themselves out.

Jennie Geiss remembered Thalia.

Thalia was dead, and Zalmox had disappeared. No one was really surprised. The first members of the *Sonderkommando Korps* had reported his ship gone after their return from dumping the first load of rotting body parts. Jennie accepted the news of his departure with the same equanimity with which she had accepted her own instinct to kill him.

They blamed him, and they knew he was not to blame. Zalmox had been the catalyst, but what moment is ever catalyst-free? Thalia had been right. No one said so aloud, of course: it was hardly necessary. Zalmox was a force to be resisted—perhaps he existed for the purpose of being resisted. Thalia had resisted, and Thalia had died. Those who had not resisted had lived, disgusted with the miasma Zalmox left in his wake. A negatively reinforced lesson: now that they had seen what lowness they were capable of, their determination to restrain it was stronger than if they had remained merely suspicious of their own capacity for destructiveness. This, at least, was their unspoken hope. Can an unseen devil ever be exorcised? Was he truly exorcised even now? They must be on their guard—for the rest of their lives.

A line from an obscure poet named Enderby floated into Jennie's mind: *Crousseau on a raft sought Johnjack's rational island*. Jean-Jacques Rousseau. Crousseau. Crusoe, reasoning nature into insular submissiveness. But in the midst of reason and enlightenment, the Pythians had lusted after unreason and endarkenment.

Generally the Pythians didn't talk much—as if speaking aloud their own unspeakableness would help cleanse away their guilt. The guilt would have to be purged eventually; but now they needed to bite down on their collective aching tooth. They concentrated on clearing the body-parts bank. Kidneys, livers, pancreases, eyes, tongues, fingers, and toes. Brains. Dr. Tirsos and his aides were working without rest to construct a new life-system; but even if they were successful, there would be no brain available to operate it. Everyone knew this. No one spoke of it.

The emergency life-support system was designed to provide a minimum of necessities for a six-week period. The supply ship wasn't due for another four months.

Jennie lay alone on her bed, fully awake during her rest period. The clean-up job was endless and she was exhausted, but she couldn't sleep. The old familiar depression had returned, magnified uncountable times by what had happened to Pythia. She hadn't even bothered asking Bert whether anything was left that might help her. She had finally forced herself to accept the fact that it was she, not Zalmox, who had raped Thalia.

The day before, Claude had found her holding a piece of broken glass over her wrist. It had taken her the better part of two hours to convince him that she'd already decided against self-destruction. He had caught her in the aftermath of shock; she didn't know how long she'd been sitting like that. Such a gesture was ridiculous under the circumstances; they could all die anyway.

They would all die, unless someone's brain was removed and placed in the new cyborg "body." And Pythia had no intention of dying. A brain was needed; a brain would be taken. But whose? Scientist, technician, experimental human, normal member of a control group—each was essential to the complete and efficient functioning of a restored Pythia. Everybody was essential.

Everybody except one person.

Jennie lay on her bed and could not sleep.

• • •

At last the body-parts bank was cleared. Then began the back-breaking chore of making the colony livable again. Machinery was sorted through in a search for what could be salvaged. Broken glass had to be gathered by hand; none of the large maintenance machines could operate without Dan's central power source. Food was a problem, the animals had to be cared for, sanitary facilities had to be improvised. Soon every gorge within walking distance was filled with Pythia's waste.

After great pain, wrote Emily Dickinson, a formal feeling comes. It was almost two weeks before the Pythians were able to start turning to each other again. Even then, the numbness, the formality, persisted.

Because it wasn't finished yet.

"Also, there's this. When Dan went, interplanetary communication went with him. We've got to warn Earth not to let Zalmox land. We don't have much time; it may already be too late. We have to reach an agreement right now."

"Well, I think putting a suicidal mind in control is nothing short of madness. Better to use one of the normals."

"The normals are all children and adolescents. An adolescent can't do Dan's work."

"Can Jennie? Can you be sure she won't pull a Feodor?"

"Can you be sure she won't destroy herself anyway? Her only chance may be atonement. She'll never totally lose her feeling of guilt. But the chance to compensate—"

"Wait a minute. We're not talking about therapy for Jennie Geiss, we're talking about the survival of Pythia."

"They're the same thing! We need an adult mind that is highly motivated to help Pythia. And I say that's Jennie Geiss."

Silence.

"What a sacrifice to ask of *anyone*."

"I don't think Jennie will see it as a sacrifice. She'll see it as a chance to . . . to pay her dues."

Another silence.

"All right," said Angelina Baker slowly. "I agree." The

other heads around the table nodded reluctantly.

"I'll tell her," said Dr. Tirsos.

"You needn't go any further," said Jennie. "I know what's coming next."

Dr. Tirsos was silent. Then: "You've already thought about this, haven't you?"

She nodded.

"Have you reached a decision?"

Jennie looked him in the eye. "Dr. Tirsos, do I have a choice?"

He looked older and more tired than she had ever seen him. "To be honest, Jennie, I don't know. We don't have any rules to follow here. What we're asking of you is abominable. But we *are* asking you. Oh, Jennie," the old man sighed, "it seems as if we're piling tragedy on tragedy. But there's nothing else to be done."

"What tragedy?" asked Jennie.

Jennie's thoughts wandered, and got lost, and wandered some more:

—Dr. Tirsos is wrong to dignify this absurd farce by calling it tragedy. Our "catharsis" hasn't settled matters; we aren't clean yet. This purging will go on for a long time. We have a lot of shit to clear away.

—As a way of obtaining "relief," catharsis is not so much a bowel movement as it is a vomiting up of what ails you. Tragedy is a poetic stomach pump, an elaborately contrived device for correcting nature's errors. Comedy is a big swig of analgesic: coat the stomach lining, protect that delicate membrane, and your precious little tum-tum won't give you any trouble.

—St. Bergson notwithstanding, comedy's work is digestive rather than intellectual. The gut as the center of all experience (comic *and* tragic) is used primarily as a food adapter, to break down bulk into metaphoric proteins, sugars, and all the rest of it that the body needs to function. If the food won't break down, then spew it up and weep or pass it out and laugh.

—Both extremes deal with the indigestible. Both vomiting and excreting are a *reaction against* the unassimilable, either through violent ejection or conversion into waste. Comedy and tragedy both deal with the "real stuff" of life? Nonsense. They deal only with what is alien and inappropriate to the life-body, not with what is inherent and essential.

—Romance? A way of tripping out, leaving London when the plague is bad, retreating to nature and preparing to survive while the rest of the world rots away. Satire? Inoculation, pure and simple (also impure and complex). Irony? Giving up and living with the pain when all the medicines have failed.

—Everything we do is done in defense against madness.

—Oedipus blinding himself in order to see. Bottom essaying the role of Pyramus. Gawain flinching from the first blow of the axe. Gulliver moving into the stables. Gregor Samsa's parents pretending they have no cockroach son. Different ways of coping with the incompatible. The healthy, unafflicted body has no need to cope: our long history of "coping" is symptomatic of—what? A terminal case of life? Sophocles, Shakespeare, the *Pearl* poet, Swift, Kafka—five brilliant diagnosticians of human *malaise*. (We also have quacks: John Fletcher, August Strindberg, Kurt Vonnegut, Pnar Muth.) But on the whole, the International/Interepochal/Inter Alia Health Service has done its job.

—But why should Thalia Boyd have been cast in the role of comic scapegoat? The new Zalmoxian society had had no place for its former leader; Thalia had become the eccentric threat to the brave new world. So inflexibly opposed to the new order was Thalia that any possibility of reconciling her to it was itself laughable. But Thalia's "exile" outrages all sense of comic fitness; the subsequent disavowing of the new order can't nullify the order's obliterating of Thalia Boyd.

—And where do I fit in? I'm no hyphenated heroine like Bel-imperia or Beatrice-Joanna. Nor am I a Melpomene to Thalia's Thalia. Our roles should have been reversed, if anything. For I am the comic outsider. Not Thalia. Not

Thalia. Yet she is the one who died.

—She died because she committed virtue—the atavistic kind that predated the belief that "virtue" is a sign something is wrong. In a good society virtues are unnecessary, the German playwright Bertolt Brecht had taught. A truly good society does not require its citizens to be heroic, or clever, or tough—because those qualities are not necessary to survival in a life that is good. And where does that kind of reformed good life exist? In the land where the Tooth Fairy dwells, ruled by the Easter Bunny and watched over by Guardian Angels. Yes, little Bertolt, there is a Santa Claus.

Jennie wondered about Thalia's method of fighting Zalmox. How easy it is to say that the best way of maintaining control is to hold a *loose* rein! Loose or tight, does it make a great deal of difference if the animal is going to run amuck anyway? Literature abounds with warnings: Make room in your life for the darker side of your nature, for ultimately there is no denying it. It will emerge, it will have its day. And then? And then it will sink back into temporary quiescence, conscious restraints having been strengthened because of the latest outburst.

But how does one "make room" for what is antithetical to all that one cherishes? Thalia had been trying to defend a *value*. For the first time the thought occurred to Jennie that Thalia must have known all along Zalmox would defeat her. Yet she'd resisted his encroachment upon her ideals, her work, her *rights*—until all Pythia had turned against her. Even then, she had said *No*.

Acknowledging the bestial in mankind is easy. Facing up to the futility of opposing it is a little harder. Opposing it *anyway* is next to impossible.

Thalia had found it possible.

Thalia was not a saint. She was a woman, take her for all in all. She was courageous—or foolhardy; principled—or obstinate; far-seeing—or naive. Even now Jennie couldn't be sure. If ever she needed that "negative capability" Keats spoke of, now was the time. Because she knew she had already made her choice; and she also knew she would live out the rest of her life without ever knowing with any certainty whether it was the right choice or not. She had chosen to repeat Thalia's *No*, and to keep repeating it as long as she had the power to do so. And the way to repeat Thalia's *No* was to say *Yes* to Dr. Tirsos.

Thalia Boyd could not be replaced. But Dan could.

So it was settled. Pythia breathed first a sigh of relief, then a prayer of thanksgiving. And then wondered how to look Jennie Geiss in the eye. Dr. Tirsos's work was almost done. In two days, three at the most, Jennie's new life would be ready for her.

Thalia was irretrievably lost. Dan was lost too—but not irretrievably. His personality had stamped itself fully on the memory tapes, blessedly stored underground and thus undamaged. So part of Dan could be retrieved, just like data. Except, of course, Dan was not just like data. He was like Dan, which is to say like no one nor anything else. There was no danger of Jennie's being submerged under a newly vitalized Dan. Jennie would remain Jennie, with the aid of whatever parts of Dan's impress she'd choose to avail herself of. It would be a union of mentalities; Jennie wryly acknowledged the fitness of Dan's becoming her permanent mate. *Let me not to the marriage of true minds admit impediments.*

Love is not love which alters when it alteration finds. Claude had attempted first to comfort Jennie, then to try to find a way of altering the inevitable. He failed at both. They would spend disquieting moments together, he staring at her—perhaps trying to visualize her in her future state. Jennie stared at him in return, trying to see him in his present state.

How was it possible to live in such intimacy with another person and then suddenly realize one had never seen beyond the stereotype? Was this Claude's problem now—that Jennie had escaped *her* stereotype and he no longer had a category through which to view her? This was something they should have come to grips with long ago.

But it didn't matter now.

Prepping finished. Movement. Overheads bright in the O.R. Figures, low voices. Anesthesia.

Numbness. Heaviness. Grayness. *Blotting everything out!*

"You're fighting it, honey," Angelina said.

Deep breaths. The gray grows heavier.

"Try concentrating on one thing." Dr. Tirsos's voice, faint.

Poetry. Recite. *Recite*:

—Little we see in nature that is ours oh god it is a fearful thing to see the human soul take wing I live not in myself but I become portion of that around me a heart how shall I say too soon made glad too easily impressed since there's no help come let us kiss and part I was half mad with beauty on that day the gaps I mean no one has seen them made or heard them made but at spring mending-time we find them there that truth should be silent I had almost forgot a land where all things always seemed the same and we are here as on a darkling plain we are not sure of sorrow and joy was never sure I do repent and yet I do despair wee sleekit cowrin tim'rous beastie on what wings dare he aspire but a tyrant spell has bound me a gaze blank and pitiless as the sun I too dislike it there are things that are important beyond all this fiddle mad in pursuit and in possession so thou shalt not kill but need'st not strive officiously to keep alive why should she give her bounty to the dead too soon dejected and too soon elate when the hurlyburly's done when the battle's lost and

SCIENCE FICTION BESTSELLERS FROM BERKLEY

Frank Herbert

DUNE   (03698-7—$2.25)

DUNE MESSIAH   (03585-9—$1.75)

CHILDREN OF DUNE   (03310-4—$1.95)

Philip José Farmer

THE FABULOUS RIVERBOAT   (03378-3—$1.50)

NIGHT OF LIGHT   (03366-X—$1.50)

TO YOUR SCATTERED BODIES GO   (03175-6—$1.75)

* * * * * * *

STRANGER IN A STRANGE LAND   (03782-7—$2.25)
  by Robert A. Heinlein

TAU ZERO   (03909-9—$1.75)
  by Poul Anderson

THE WORD FOR WORLD IS FOREST   (03466-6—$1.75)
  by Ursula K. Le Guin

SLAN   (03851-3—$1.50)
  by A.E. van Vogt

THE MAN IN THE HIGH CASTLE   (03908-0—$1.75)
  by Philip K. Dick

THE STARS MY DESTINATION   (03745-2—$1.75)
  by Alfred Bester

Send for a list of all our books in print.

These books are available at your local bookstore, or send price indicated plus 30¢ for postage and handling. If more than four books are ordered, only $1.00 is necessary for postage. Allow three weeks for delivery. Send orders to:

Berkley Book Mailing Service
P.O. Box 690
Rockville Centre, New York 11570